A HUSTLER'S WORLD

A Gripping Urban Fiction Tale of Crime, Loyalty, and Street Survival

L A RUN

1

It was a normal day like any other as Keebler casually stepped out of Denny's restaurant and into the crisp Memphis air. After quickly scanning the area for anything out of the ordinary, he felt it was safe to leave.

"I need a come up," he said to himself as he made his way to his car.

Going into his pocket for his keys, he looked at his small wad of money. As he hit the alarm on his 2002 Crown Victoria, he knew his bankroll was about to get smaller due to the fact that he had to get some gas, and this caused him to shake his head. No one would've thought Keebler was struggling when judging by the big wheels on his car. The Crown Victoria was sitting on 26-inch chrome floaters that shined in the sunlight that reflected off the bowling ball blue paint job that glistened with gold specks.

Just as Keebler got comfortable and started the car, movement caught his eyesight. The money-green Beamer M6 Coupe sitting on 24-inch rims made sure it demanded everyone's attention. It certainly had

Keebler's undivided attention as he pulled into traffic to follow the exotic vehicle. It was already understood who was behind the wheel of the BMW. Godzilla was considered the number two man in the eastside drug ring, and he was a known killer. He didn't ride with tinted windows because he loved to beef in the streets and was quick on the trigger.

Keebler was aware of all these things, so he took them into consideration while contemplating what he was about to attempt. His plan was just to follow the drug dealer in hopes of finding out something that would help him get paid at a later time, but if any type of opportunity that would allow him to get at the man right quick presented itself, he was ready for that also.

Driving casually down Winchester, Godzilla continued flexing through traffic until he got to Clarke Road. He made a left turn into a neighborhood and turned down a couple of side streets until he reached his destination. The car he parked behind belonged to another dopeboy who worked for Godzilla. Comfortable with his hustle, the young dopeboy never paid any attention to what was going on around him. If he did, he would have spotted the custom blue Crown Victoria parking at the curb a few houses down the street. Without a care in the world, Godzilla went inside the house.

"This shit is too easy," Keebler said to himself as he continued watching the spot.

At first, he didn't know how to take the home, since the neighborhood they were in was high middle-classed. After thirty minutes of scoping, it seemed like everything came to life. Other custom vehicles pulled up and were leaving minutes later, confirming that the house was used solely as a traphouse. He was like a kid in a candy store as he watched the spot and realized how easy it would be for him to go in and get everything. It was like the door stayed open for all.

Because he didn't want to have to deal with Godzilla unless it was necessary, Keebler patiently waited until the dopeboy finally decided to leave before attempting anything. When the Beamer sped past, Keebler ducked and watched the BMW go on about its business. Another car pulled up at the house just as he decided to make the hit, causing Keebler to hesitate. For some reason, it felt like the man who'd just gone in the house was taking forever. Despite his intuition telling him he should wait, Keebler decided it was now or never and resolved to lay down whoever was in the house as he quietly but quickly jumped out of his car with two Glock 40s in hands.

Without warning, Keebler ran up to the front door and turned the knob to find it unlocked.

"Unbelievable," Keebler told himself as he entered the house.

Two male voices could be heard from the next room, and it sounded like money was the topic of conversation. Keebler closed and locked the door while listening to his future victims discuss business.

"Is this the same work I got last time?" one voice asked.

"Yep! That shit went fast, didnt it?" the other voice said proudly.

Keebler listened for as long as he could before he felt the time was right. After counting down from five, he sprang into action.

"Just pack everything up, and I'll take the shit off your hands," Keebler said while pointing a Glock 40 in the face of both men.

At first, neither man moved. They looked at Keebler like he'd lost his mind by trying to rob the spot of the biggest dopeboy in the area.

"I don't like repeating myself," Keebler said, then hit the man who came to buy dope across the head. The man was out cold, so he pointed both pistols to the man running the trap house. "But for you, I'll make one exception. Pack this shit up... *Now!*" Keebler stated firmly.

"Pack it yourself. I only work for..." the dopeboy was saying but never finished his statement because he heard shots.

Bloc!... Bloc!... Bloc!

All three shots hit their target, instantly killing the man who came to spend money. The look in Keebler's eyes said everything as he stared at the man and watched his attitude change instantly. He quickly loaded up the nine ounces of cocaine he was in the midst of selling, along with the money the man had brought to purchase the drugs.

Once everything was loaded, the dopeboy told him that was everything in the house, unaware that the house had been watched. Keebler knew there was more, but after looking at what he was getting from the spur of the moment lick, he was content with what he had. Keebler hit the man twice over the head with his pistol. Hearing the man snoring, he casually picked up the duffel bag and headed out the front door. His heart was beating fast as he looked around to see if the shots had been heard by neighbors. As far as he could tell, nobody had heard anything.

Once he was safely back inside his own vehicle, a smile spread across his face. The same car he'd followed to the spot came speeding by on its way back to the house.

"This is the reason why I ride behind tint," Keebler said as he watched the customized BMW park in the yard. It was like Godzilla could feel that he was being watched because just as he was about to go in the house, he stopped and looked around.

"Yeah, you escaped this time," Keebler said as he openly watched the man from inside his car.

When he didn't see anything out of the ordinary, Godzilla went on in the house. Keebler watched and waited until the front door was closed before backing all the way up the street and turning around. He made sure to remember the street name and address because he had a feeling he'd be back for another visit. His mind was on coming back and getting the rest of the work as he was still laughing at how they had slipped. In reality, Keebler had been the one slipping. He was in such a rush to make the lick that he paid no attention to the surveillance cameras that were not just sitting outside the house, but inside the house as well. This meant that Keebler's face was all over the system.

As soon as Godzilla entered the house and heard how quiet it was, he knew something was wrong. Quickly upping the .44 Bulldog from his waist holster, he went into predator mode as he silently headed to the room where his best friend Calvin usually conducted business. Before he even got to the room, the smell of death filled his nostrils, and he began thinking the worst. Godzilla already had it in his mind that whoever violated his space would pay, but if his best friend was dead, he would bring hell to the entire city.

As he entered the room, he spotted two bodies laid out on the floor. Seeing Calvin almost made Godzilla lose his cool until the man started moving. As he slowly came to, he grabbed his head, moaning and shaking it so he could regain his vision. The first thing he noticed once everything became clear was Godzilla standing over him with a huge smile on his face.

"What's so damn funny?" Calvin asked as he slowly got up off the floor. For a quick moment, he'd forgot what had happened until he spotted the dead body on the floor.

"You let a nigga creep in on you," Godzilla spoke, still smiling. "I told you about trusting niggas," he continued as he shook his head.

Calvin thought about the robbery and the fact that the intruder had the audacity to not wear a mask. In his eyes, that was like calling him and his crew pussies, and that was something they were not.

"We gotta get rid of this body," Calvin said suddenly, now back to his old self.

"I'm already on top of it," Godzilla said while pulling out his iPhone. As he spoke on the phone, he led the way to the back bedroom where the surveillance monitors were. This was also the room where Calvin stashed the drugs he hadn't sold yet. The room was still in perfect order, letting Godzilla know that whoever ran in the house hadn't done a thorough search of the premises. In his eyes, that meant they were amateurs, which meant they would be easy to locate and kill.

The call Godzilla made was quick, and he ended it just as he sat at the monitors and began rewinding video. He wanted to know who they were, what they drove, and if they'd slipped up some kind of way, which would narrow the search and retaliation down.

"What did the nigga get?" Godzilla asked while watching a lone stranger rush up to the front door. He kept rewinding the video in an attempt to find out more about the robber.

"A quarter brick that belonged to Shorty Bud. Almost ten stacks that was Junebug's," Calvin explained while watching the monitor with his best friend.

"You know we gotta keep this lil' incident between us," Godzilla stated firmly. "If Shorty Bud finds out you got caught slipping, he may put a price on both of our heads," he continued. Godzilla's facial expression said it all, so Calvin quickly agreed. They both continued looking at the surveillance video, trying to put everything together.

It was a known fact that Godzilla was a dangerous man, but he wasn't the big dog of the streets. While the streets feared him, there lay a more dangerous force in the background that nobody suspected. Shorty Bud was a crazy, notorious drug dealer who made his rise in the game by being on the frontline of all the action as he came up. A rumor once spread that he lived so recklessly that a bet was made between Shorty Bud and another dopeboy who had the connect at the time. The bet was that Shorty Bud would not go to rival territory and kill an adversary who had been trying to move in on the drug dealer. He was told that the reward would be an introduction to the drug connect.

Shorty Bud supposedly went through the area not only killing his target but everybody down with the target.

The drug dealer kept his word and took Shorty Bud to meet his plug, which was a group of men of Spanish descent. After hearing how Shorty Bud handled the business, they made him a proposal that would change his life forever. Being the killer he was, Shorty Bud accepted the assignment, which was to kill the dopeboy. The plug felt that the man they were currently dealing with was an informant, and if his back was ever pushed against the wall, he would rat them out. After hearing the reason for the hit, Shorty Bud decided to take it upon himself to show niggas how he moved. He ended up whacking the dopeboy in front of the plug.

"I hate rats," Shorty Bud told the plug and left them to deal with the body. That was a day he never regretted, and the man had still been killing ever since.

As Keebler sped away from the scene, he was so excited about the robbery that he'd forgotten that he needed gas until his car started to sputter just as he crossed over Mendenhall while headed back in the direction of the Denny's restaurant.

"Shit!" Keebler yelled and yanked the wheel to the right, pulling into the BP gas station at the corner. Since he'd lost power, he just coasted up to the first available gas pump.

"May as well fill it up," Keebler stated excitedly as he jumped out the car. He quickly put the gas nozzle in his car and strutted into the store to find the female cashier openly admiring him.

"Let it fill up for me while I grab a few things shawty," Keebler said just as his Blackberry started ringing. Looking at the number, he smiled as he answered the call.

"Krash! What up, nigga?" Keebler said to his right-hand man.

"Where the fuck you at?" Krash asked in his deep voice. As bad as Keebler wanted to speak about the lick he'd just made, he never discussed business over any type of electronic frequencies.

"Even if I told you what just happened, you wouldn't believe me, but I'm on my way to you now," Keebler replied.

Krash knew then that his friend been on the grind and hated that he'd missed out. "How long before you get to me?" he asked.

"I'm leaving the eastside now, so give me about fifteen to twenty minutes to get to you," Keebler replied as he reached the counter with a 20-ounce Icehouse, a Big Grab bag of Chili Cheese Fritos and king-size Snickers candy bar.

"Bet that," Krash replied and ended the call.

"Your gas has stopped pumping," the cashier said in a sweet voice that caught Keebler's attention. He looked up, and it was like he was noticing the brown-skinned beauty for the first time.

"How about you add all this shit up?" Keebler said cockily. "Put a carton of Newport shorts and your phone number with that," he continued with a smile as the two held eye contact.

She completed the transaction and placed the items in a bag. Keebler quickly looked through the bag like he was missing something. Just as he was about to ask about the number again, there was a piece of paper in his face.

"Make sure you use it," the female said seductively.

Keebler took the paper and looked at the name. "Zya," he said as he leaned over the counter to get a look at her body. Without saying a word, he wrote his cell number down. "Call me when you about to get off," Keebler demanded as he set the number down, then left without waiting for a reply.

Once Keebler was situated in his car, he sat there letting it run while he went into his bag of goodies. Pulling out an ounce of powder cocaine, he took a crispy hundred-dollar bill and folded it before stuffing it with powder. He glanced back inside the store to find his new friend watching the car although she couldn't see inside. When he hit a button on the remote control, so much bass tried to escape the huge kickbox in the trunk that he knew everything in the store was rattling. After carefully crushing the powder, Keebler took his pinky nail and dug in, putting two considerable piles up each nostril and sniffing away. The immediate drain let the man know how potent the drug was. After grabbing a cigarette from his already opened pack, Keebler lit it while nodding his head to the Yo Gotti's CD before pulling off, knowing all eyes were on him.

2

While chilling by the lakeside in the backyard of his Coro Lake home, Krash was blazing up a blunt. Sitting in his lap was a twenty-dollar bill stuffed with powder cocaine. Just as he took a long pull from the blunt, he could hear bass from a distance. By the time the sounds were in front of his house, Krash already knew who it was.

"Keebler's crazy ass is out here knocking shit off the walls again," Krash's fiancée Trina yelled out the patio door.

"Let him know I'm back here," Krash yelled over his shoulder without even looking back. He could hear the patio door closing only to be opened again a minute later before the sound of footsteps approached in his freshly cut yard.

"What's wrong with sis?" Keebler asked as he gave Krash dap before sitting down next to him.

"Besides the fact that every time you pull up, you knocking pictures down?" Krash asked jokingly. Truth be told, he had the exact same sound system in his car. They were so close that they both owned 2002 Crown Victorias with 26-inch floaters. The only difference in the vehicles was the custom paint jobs. Where Keebler had the bowling ball blue candy paint, Krash had candy apple red paint.

"On the real, though, she been trippin' about us not going out as much anymore," Krash admitted before taking a small pile of powder to each nostril. "Between the mortgage and other bills, plus me trying to keep her looking good, money been kinda tight lately," he continued.

Instead of replying, Keebler went into the duffel bag, knowing his friend was watching him closely. "Hopefully this should tide you over until we can get back on our feet," Keebler said before pulling out four of the nine ounces of cocaine he took in the lick. Before Krash could speak, Keebler pulled out three bundles of one-hundred-dollar bills and tossed them to him.

"What the fuck you been up to today?" Krash asked.

Keebler told him about how his day had been going up until he'd seen Godzilla riding in traffic. He told him about how he followed the man and ended up robbing one of his spots.

"Fool! You robbed Godzilla?" Krash asked with a smile.

"He wasn't there when I actually ran up in the spot, but the nigga I got was his boy Calvin," Keebler replied nonchalantly.

Krash just shook his head because he already knew what could possibly come behind the robbery. "You know who dude work for, right?" Krash asked, now serious. He was trying to figure out the easiest way to tell his homeboy that he may now have a hit on his head.

"Honestly, Krash, I could care less about him or who he works for," Keebler admitted. "I know how Godzilla gets down, but on the same token, you already know how to roll myself," he continued before pulling out one of his Glocks.

"You already know whatever the outcome is, I got your back. But just so you don't be in the dark about shit, I want you to know what we may be up against," Krash stated. "That's Shorty Bud's right-hand man," he continued.

Just hearing the name Shorty Bud would make any man think, and that was what Keebler was now doing. After a quick minute, he shrugged his shoulders.

"That nigga bleed just like me," Keebler replied, then pulled out the dollar bill he had filled with cocaine. Instantly, his mind went back to the woman at the BP. "I met a goddess who may just be my future wife at a gas station after the lick," Keebler said with a smile.

As he described her, Krash could see a sparkle in his friend's eyes that wasn't there at first. As he listened, an idea came to mind that could help Keebler get his girl, as well as get Krash back in good with his own girl.

***

Out in East Memphis, the dopeboy who was killed in the traphouse had been dumped across town in his car so he wouldn't be linked to them when he was found. Now, Godzilla was back in traffic and trying to put a name to the face he had on a printed sheet of paper. He had to admit to himself that he liked how the unknown man didn't think twice about going up in the house. If the circumstances had been different, he would've been trying to put the man on the team. Unfortunately, the robber had crossed the line by taking from him, and in Godzilla's eyes, the penalty for that was death.

"I know how to handle this shit," Godzilla told himself after he'd been riding around for a couple of hours asking other hustlers if they knew the face on paper, only to come up emptyhanded.

He suddenly realized he had an appetite, so Godzilla pulled up at the Sonic on Perkins Road and parked as close as he could to the restaurant. Before handling his business, he pressed the red button where orders were placed.

"Welcome to Sonic! How may I help you today?" a female asked cheerfully.

Godzilla couldn't help but smile at how hyper the woman sounded. He quickly placed his order, then rolled up his window as he went through directory in his iPhone for the number he was looking for.

After pressing Call, he silently waited for the voice he was looking to hear.

"Yeah," a voice came through the phone.

"What it do?" Godzilla asked with a smile.

"Just getting up for the day," the man replied.

Godzilla already knew this, which was why he waited to call. The man he was speaking to was named Dirty, and his hustle was murder. At 24 years old, he didn't have any friends but was very well known. Usually, if he popped up lingering in a hood, it was best that everyone left because nine times out of ten, somebody was about to die. It was because of this Dirty usually stayed in until nightfall.

"I got something I need checked out for me," Godzilla stated.

"You know I'm always up for a job," Dirty replied. "Especially when it's niggas like you paying me," he continued. Before another word was said, a picture was sent to Dirty's text messages, and he almost lost his breath when he saw who the picture was of.

"Are you familiar with this cat?" Godzilla asked.

"Nah, I don't know him," Dirty replied.

He was glad at that moment that the conversation was over the phone because he knew for sure that Godzilla would've read his body language and known he was lying. Then he would have been put in a situation he did not want to be in.

"What's up wit' him?" Dirty asked.

Godzilla told him about how Keebler had disrespected his personal space by robbing his traphouse. "I got five stacks to find out who he is and where he rests, and ten to send him to hell on a first-class flight," Godzilla explained just as a young female stepped to his window with his food in hand. He paid the young lady and let his window back up without stopping the conversation.

"How many people know about this?" Dirty asked.

"You already know that you'll always be my first choice," Godzilla replied, letting the man know that nobody knew his intentions.

"Let me get myself together and I'm on it," Dirty stated.

"Keep me posted," Godzilla said and ended the call.

As Dirty sat there looking at the picture in his phone, he couldn't help but shake his head. He was trying to figure out how to tell a man he considered to be his big brother that a hit was on his head when a soft yawn got his attention. Laying in the bed beside him was his girlfriend Midnight.

"What's wrong, baby?" she asked upon seeing that the love of her life had something going on in his mind. Without verbally replying, Dirty turned his iPhone to allow her to see the picture on the screen. "What's going on?" Midnight asked, instantly recognizing the face as she sat up in the bed, exposing her size 34C breasts. She had nipples the size of .38 bullets, and at the moment, they were pointing at Dirty, demanding his attention.

"There's a hit on his head," Dirty replied, but his eyes were on his love's big breasts.

"Who did it?" Midnight asked seriously.

"Godzilla," he replied.

At first, Midnight wanted to get her freak on before their night started, but hearing that name changed everything.

"We have to go deal with this now," she said as she jumped out of bed and ran to the bathroom, giving Dirty a clear view of her huge butt as it shook.

People would look at Dirty and Midnight and think they were a young college couple by first appearances. They both always dressed casual but expensively in name brand clothing and drove around town in a BMW 650i. The fact that the car was black on black let those in the streets know not to take them lightly. Behind that college student persona lay the deadliest up-and-coming hit team to ever hit the hood. They were quick to set up dealers, using Midnight as bait since there weren't too many men living who could resist the darkness of her complexion. Standing barely over five feet tall and weighing 138 pounds in all the right places, she was a woman who'd have any man doing a double take. Her special quality was her natural deep green eyes that seemed to glow off her deep-chocolate skin, which was why everyone called her Midnight.

Twenty minutes later, the black BMW 650i was in traffic and on the hunt.

"Do you know where he is?" Midnight asked as Dirty whipped the Beamer through the evening traffic.

"Not really, but since he hit a spot in the east, and I know how Keebler gets down, I say we start in that area," Dirty thought aloud. He knew how Keebler and Krash liked to frequent the strip clubs, with one in particular. Without another word being said, Dirty unmuted the system and let Lil Boosie flood the vehicle.

***

After Krash told him the idea he had, Keebler couldn't help but smile.

"Y'all may need to go get dressed then because I'm supposed to pick her up from work when she gets off, which should be very shortly," Keebler said while checking the time on his iPhone and considering that it was almost time for the third shift hour.

Krash immediately went in the house to get fresh and tell his girl Trina to do the same. Since Keebler had a few minutes to spare, he pushed a couple of small piles of powder up his nose, then pulled the piece of paper out of his pocket. He dialed the numbers into the phone, then pushed the speakerphone button. As the phone rang, he quickly snorted some more powder.

"Hello," a sweet voice that sounded like an angel to Keebler answered.

"What's up, Zya?" Keebler asked, trying to sound sexy himself.

"I was just about to call you and see if you could come scoop me up," Zya said, getting straight to the point. Her forwardness kind of caught the man off guard, but he quickly bounced back.

"Ain't that some shit? I was just calling to see if you wanted to kick it tonight," Keebler said.

They spoke for a few minutes, acting like kids in high school, before both agreed that Keebler would pick her up, and they would go out for a late-night bite to eat. Zya had a few customers come in the gas station, so he let her go but promised that he was on his way to her.

Ten minutes after he ended the call, both Krash and Trina stepped outside dressed to impress.

"I see you, lil sis," Keebler said before standing up to meet them.

In the back of his mind, he still didn't see how his best friend managed to get a woman like that. Krash claimed he couldn't see the resemblance, but everybody else who looked at Trina had to look twice. She looked exactly like Lisa Raye, and she was known to turn heads. Keebler could see that tonight wouldn't be any different.

As they all headed to the cars, Keebler was surprised to see them walk to their ride.

"We'll follow you to give you and your new friend time to get acquainted," Krash said with a smile.

"You think your old ass can keep up? You know I like to flex," Keebler asked jokingly.

"I taught your ass how to flex, fool," Krash said and jumped in his car.

Moments later, both Crown Victorias were speeding off down the street. It didn't take Dirty long to get to the east side. For some reason, this was the area everybody came to when they wanted to have a good time. The best of everything was in the area: clubs, strip clubs, after-hour hangouts, and some of the sexiest women in the city.

Without wasting time, the Beamer pulled up to Cabaret and slowly cruised the lot. They were looking for the customized Crown Victoria, and there were only two in the city with a specific paint job, so they knew it would not be hard to spot. After making two slow trips around the entire lot, it was understood that if he didn't find Keebler roaming through one of the hoods nearby, they would have to call the man. As the Beamer made its way toward Winchester, Dirty spotted something that made him smile.

"Look, sweetheart," he said and nodded at the gas station across the street. Sitting in the turning lane with the wheel turned and shining off the light poles lining Winchester wasn't just one Crown Vic, but both, making traffic slow down to look at them.

"I see he still doesn't know how to lay low," Midnight said as she shook her head.

Dirty sat and waited to see where his play brother was going before pulling down on him. When traffic finally stopped moving, Keebler flexed up on BP's lot, already knowing he was being watched. He only hoped Krash stuck to the script and flexed with him, but he already knew he was.

By the time they pulled up at the gas pumps, Zya was already stepping outside looking more beautiful than Keebler could remember. She had a face like Megan Good, a body like Taraji P. Henson, and a walk that could have had its own theme music. For a moment, he just sat there and stared with a smile as she casually floated to the passenger side door. Just as she hopped in and closed the door, Keebler was quickly brought back to reality when his car was blocked off by the black Beamer 650. Zya's eyes immediately got big, thinking they were about to be robbed or carjacked when she saw the light-skinned man with dreadlocks hop out the car.

"Be cool, shorty. That's just my baby brother," Keebler said and hopped out to meet with Dirty.

Before anything could be said, Krash eased up on the group, already expecting the worst. The smile Dirty had on his face seemed to take away the worry of what was about to be said, but the look in his eyes let Keebler know that the youngster had some serious business to discuss. Dirty quickly dapped up with both men to show them that his love was still there.

"You know you can't be riding down on niggas like that," Keebler said.

"I couldn't risk you pulling off on me before I got the chance to get at y'all," Dirty replied.

"What's that urgent that you couldn't just call?" Krash asked, but in his heart, he already knew the issue. Instead of replying, Dirty pulled out his phone and showed them the picture that had been sent to him.

3

The color immediately drained from Keebler's face as he stared at the picture of himself wearing the same clothes he was currently wearing.

"I can't believe I slipped like that," Keebler said, talking mainly to himself but loud enough that they could hear. He stared at the picture a moment longer before regaining his composure.

"So, you already know where this came from and who sent it to me, right?" Dirty asked. Keebler just nodded for a reply. "At this time, I'm the only nigga who knows dude got a hit on your head," Dirty said. He explained that if he didn't handle the business within the next three days, Godzilla would spread the word around town about the hit.

"So, what's the ticket on my head?" Keebler asked.

"Five for your whereabouts and ten to do you in," Dirty said.

"So, we got three days to get at dude before he puts the word out," Krash spoke. Dirty nodded and smiled at the same time.

"What's so funny?" Keebler asked. He'd known the young hitman since he was little, so he knew when Dirty was up to something.

"Bruh, dude has given me a lot of business in the past," Dirty stated firmly. "I say that to say, for the right price, I'll bring dude to you," he continued.

"How much?" Krash asked before Keebler could speak. He already knew how important it was to get at Godzilla before word got around town about the hit.

"Give me twenty grand, and you got yourself a deal," Dirty replied.

"Bet," Keebler said.

"I'll get at you later on with the instructions on where he'll be," Dirty said, then gave both men dap again. Keebler watched as his lil brother jumped back in his car and sped off into the night before he turned to his best friend.

"We gotta get on our hustle," Keebler said.

"We can always get on the plan I had," Krash said.

Keebler stared off into the night, thinking about everything for a minute. "Fuck it! Let's do it," Keebler replied as he gave Krash dap. They glanced back at both vehicles, remembering the two sexy ladies waiting on them, then went to enjoy themselves on a night out.

***

"So, what did bruh say?" Midnight asked as they sped up Mendenhall.

"He gone give me twenty racks to set Godzilla up," Dirty replied nonchalantly.

Midnight looked at her man with a straight face. "Do he even have twenty-thousand dollars?" she asked.

"I don't know," Dirty answered. "This is Keebler and Krash we're talking about. Plus, he just hit Godzilla, which is why he is hot now. With that being said, I don't put shit past bruh, and I'll always ride with him," he continued.

"So, what're we doing tonight?" Midnight asked.

"Getting about that paper," Dirty said while making a left turn onto Knight Arnold and speeding up the street.

For a moment, Midnight didn't know what was going on, but she was on alert because of how fast Dirty was going. Then she got a glimpse of the taillights in front of them.

"Don't let them get away," Midnight said while admiring the new blue Cadillac CT6 sitting on 26-inch chrome wheels. With no tinted windows on the car, they could clearly see the two men inside smoking on a blunt.

"I got this. You just be ready to do your thang," Dirty said while being careful not to lose their next target.

As soon as the first opportunity presented itself, which was minutes later, Midnight was up to the plate. The Cadillac pulled up at a shopping center and parked. As Dirty found a spot to park, he noticed the passenger get out and walk into a tobacco discount store.

"Go do your thing, baby," he told Midnight as he gave her the car keys. "I'm getting this fool and taking the car. I know a nigga who will give us something nice for those rims," he continued when Midnight looked at him funny.

Before she could protest, Dirty was out of the BMW, creeping between other vehicles, and headed toward his victim. Midnight already knew what was about to go down, so she got out the car and walked seductively toward the tobacco store. Even though it was dark outside, she knew that whoever was out was now watching her, and the man in the Cadillac was no exception.

The man in the Cadillac sat straight up when he saw the dark-skinned goddess who was walking toward the tobacco store. As he watched Midnight go into the store, he debated on whether to go get at her, unaware that he was being watched as well until it was too late. Before he knew what was going on, the passenger side door popped open, and Dirty hopped in with his .10mm cocked and pointed. To show his victim that he was serious, Dirty shot the man in the leg to make sure he had his undivided attention.

"You know what this is, so give it up and get out," Dirty demanded.

The man was in so much pain that he didn't put up a fight. He immediately went in his pocket and pulled out a bankroll that actually surprised Dirty. Without having to be told the man opened the door to get out which put a smirk on Dirty's face. Just as the man thought he was safe, Dirty shot him in the ass and laughed as he quickly climbed into the driver's seat and pulled off, leaving his victim laid out in the parking lot.

Midnight went into the tobacco store and did a quick look around like she was really thinking about buying something. She smiled at the old white man standing behind the cash register and silently counted to ten before turning around and leaving. She knew by that time, her man had already found his victim slipping, so she casually headed back to the car. Just as she got behind the wheel and started the BMW, she spotted the new Cadillac as it sped up Perkins Road.

"That nigga working quick," Midnight said to herself as she pulled off. The dude who was inside the tobacco store had just come outside to find his friend laid out in the parking space where the Cadillac was once parked. Without stopping, Midnight cruised by the men on her way to meet up with Dirty.

*　　　*　　　*

The first place Keebler led the way to was South Memphis to get some good weed to smoke on. Zya had said she knew someone out east who sold weed, but Keebler stressed that nobody in the town had the type of weed his homeboy had. Plus, Godzilla wasn't known to hang out on the southside, so the chances of them bumping in each other out there were slim. The two had already gotten comfortable with each other, and Keebler forgot Krash was following them until he just happened to glance in his rearview mirror just as he was turning onto the street he was looking for.

"There go my nigga right there," Keebler said as he cruised toward a group of young hustlers standing out in a front yard.

As both Crown Vics pulled up to the curb, Zya noticed as a tall, slim, dark-skinned man with long braids step away from the group. The smile on his face let the lady know he was who Keebler was coming to meet, but it was the mouth full of shiny gold teeth that got her attention.

"I'll be right back sexy," Keebler told Zya and hopped out the car to find Krash waiting on him. They both went to where the man was calmly waiting at and dapped him.

"What up, youngster?" Keebler greeted.

"You already know the business," the man replied.

"Let me get a zip of that blueberry you sold me last time, Flea," Keebler said.

"Let me get one too," Krash said before Flea could reply. Instead of replying, Flea dipped off behind the house they were standing out in front of, only to return a couple of minutes later.

"Just give me two-fifty each," Flea said before giving each man a Ziploc bag stuffed with weed that had a super strong aroma. They paid Flea and jumped back in their whips.

"Twist one up," Keebler told Zya as he watched her facial expression once she looked at the weed.

By the time Zya had the first blunt rolled up, the smooth sounds of Marvin Gaye were flooding the vehicle.

"So, what do you do?" Zya asked as she passed the blunt after taking a few pulls herself.

"I'm a small-time hustler," Keebler said calmly. They were headed toward downtown Memphis, and he was starting to get hungry. Remembering that he hadn't eaten since before he pulled that lick, he figured it was time to stop somewhere.

"You doing more than small-time hustling, baby," Zya said as she reached for the blunt. "You rolling big boy, and that's a big boy bankroll in your pocket," she continued, letting Keebler know that she was a good observer.

"Let's just say I'm small in the game right now, but things about to take a turn for the better real soon," Keebler replied with a smile. The Hydro was starting to take effect on both of them, and they both started laughing for no reason.

*****

In the car behind them, the atmosphere was totally different. As Krash followed his best friend, his lady Trina had her head in his lap gobbling his nine-inch rod like it was the last meal she would ever have. The way she was feeling had her not only trying to stuff herself with the whole nine inches, but Trina tried to put his balls in her mouth as well.

"Damn! That shit feels good," Krash moaned as he forced his eyes to stay on the road. He didn't have any idea where Keebler was headed, but he prayed that they stopped soon. Krash could feel himself about to explode, so he tried thinking about other things to prolong the eruption. Forcing himself to look at his surroundings, Krash noticed that they were heading toward downtown.

"Shit! I'm about to cum, baby," Krash yelled out suddenly.

Trina went back down on his nine inches and prepared to swallow the load her man was shooting in her mouth. The car swerved a little as Krash released the tension that had built up within him over time. Trina made sure to swallow all the protein before relaxing back in her seat with a smile on her face.

"I owe you, baby," Krash said with a smile. Instead of giving a reply, Trina rolled up a blunt and lit it.

***

"What the…" Keebler said to himself when he saw Krash swerve behind him then quickly regain control. He knew that swerve anywhere and couldn't do anything but smile because he knew his best friend was in another world at the moment. Though he wasn't really looking for it, Keebler spotted a Dixie Cafe sign on Third Street and found parking spaces where both cars would be behind each other and visible.

"You ready to meet my family?" Keebler asked.

"Sure, baby," Zya said while rubbing his arm. She was high, and the seductive look she gave almost made Keebler forget about food and head to the nearest hotel.

Holding the urge, he got out and casually strutted to the curb where Zya was waiting after she got out. As they headed to the restaurant, Krash and Trina followed. It was dark outside, and the restaurant was almost empty, so the hostess quickly found them a booth with a view of the downtown traffic. A waiter quickly approached and took their orders, then left them to get acquainted.

***

Not too far from the downtown area, Dirty was pulling up at a traphouse his cousin Twin had on lock. The house was surrounded by men of all ages who all stood admiring the two custom vehicles as he and Midnight pulled up and headed behind the house. By the time Dirty stepped out of the Cadillac, Twin was already standing there shaking his head at his cousin.

"What are you shaking your head for?" Dirty asked.

"Because I see you still at it," Twin replied.

The cousins hugged before Dirty got down to business. "You wanna cop these wheels?" he asked while pointing to the big wheels on the car.

"Damn, cuz! You like two days too late. I just put some wheels on my Cutlass," Twin explained.

"That's cool. Find me a junkie to snatch them off right quick," Dirty said as he headed to the trunk. He opened the trunk and checked out the huge speakers and the three amps mounted inside.

"Now, I will take that off your hands if it's for sale!" Twin exclaimed.

"Give me twelve hundred for the whole car, minus the wheels," Dirty stated.

Twin did a once over on the new Cadillac and knew he could make a few thousand off the motor and customized all-white leather interior, so he made the deal.

To Dirty's surprise, it took the junkie Twin had found no time to pull the wheels off the Cadillac. Once all four wheels were safely in the backseat of the BMW, Dirty had Midnight park on the street while he paid the junkie.

"What I owe you?" he asked.

"Just fuck with me, young blood," the junkie said, trying to sound cool. Dirty gave the man a one-hundred-dollar bill and watched as his eyes lit up. As Dirty got ready to leave, he was stopped by his cousin.

"Blow one with me before you dip off, cuz," Twin said with a fat blunt in his hand.

"Come on," Dirty stated then led the way to the front of the house. He'd gotten everything he wanted from the car. Now, the last thing he needed was to get caught up by the police. Plus, he didn't like the idea of leaving Midnight sitting in the car alone, considering the neighborhood they were in.

***

By the time the two couples had finished dining, they were all comfortable and getting to know each other. Trina and Zya had become good friends, which, in Keebler eyes, was a good thing. They were about to cause havoc throughout the city, and when it came time to battle, knowing Zya would be somewhere safe with someone he trusted put the man's nerves at ease.

When the waiter stepped over to the table with the check, both men reached for it. They both laughed at the gesture but neither man let the check go.

"After what you did for me today, I insist," Krash stated. Zya just watched the men with a smile on her face as she noticed how much they acted like brothers.

With a nod, Keebler released the check and turned his attention to Zya. "So, you chilling with me tonight?" he asked.

"Don't take this the wrong way, but I don't sleep around on the first date," Zya explained. She silently hoped that her decision wouldn't run Keebler off because she was really starting to like the man.

"Well, in that case, let me get you home," Keebler replied with a smile before the two couples got up to leave together.

***

Out in North Memphis, Dirty sat on the hood of his car and smoked two blunts with his cousin Twin, who made money all the while. Midnight sat in the Beamer playing on the phone while patiently waiting. She knew how her man got down in the streets, and she was cool with it. That was why they got along so well.

After the second blunt was gone, Dirty decided it was time to roll out. He said his goodbye to his cousin, then hopped in the passenger seat of the BMW.

"Let's call it a night, baby," Dirty said, then pushed the seat back.

4

Word about the robbery and carjacking Dirty pulled off the night before was spreading through the hood, not because of the police but because of the fact that the man who had been shot twice by Dirty was a mid-level dopeboy who got his work from Godzilla. Back at the traphouse, Calvin and Godzilla were discussing what was being said on the streets.

"Who do you think hit up ole T-Rock?" Godzilla asked.

"I don't know," Calvin replied. "At first, I thought that maybe the dude who hit us probably got him, but when I heard that he got shot twice, one being in the ass, I knew it had to be more personal," he continued.

"Speaking of personal," Godzilla said and pulled out his iPhone. He looked for a specific number and called.

***

Soft moans could be heard from under the covers as Midnight headed toward the galaxy of pleasure. Dirty was between her legs licking and sucking away on the treasure chest that would soon pay him with the floods of liquid gold he yearned for. Sticking his tongue in and out of her box like a key unlocking a door while rubbing on Midnight's swollen clit had the black goddess ready to climb the walls as she fought the urge to climax all over her lover's face.

"That's it right there," Midnight moaned when Dirty started sucking on her clit. Before he knew what was happening, she grabbed his head and held on as she screamed while climaxing in his mouth. Dirty continued sucking on her clit throughout the entire climax, almost causing Midnight to pass out from the overwhelming pleasure.

The phone started ringing just as Midnight came back to earth. "Let it ring, baby,"

Midnight moaned as she sat up in the bed. She looked so good to Dirty, and the way his nine-inch rod stood at attention revealed what was on his mind. Before Dirty could answer, Midnight pushed him down on the bed and climbed on top of him as she prepared to straddle her man. The heat coming from her body sent Dirty over the hill as she guided his penis into her hole, causing him to moan. They both started moving, and before they knew it, the phone ringing was drowned out by the sound of their bodies smacking into each other.

Dirty grabbed Midnight's ass, spreading her butt cheeks apart to allow him to go deeper. Feeling the spot he was hoping for, Dirty pushed in and out of her with a demanding force and speed.

"Oh, shit, baby! I'm cu- I'm cumming!" Midnight yelled as she held on to the headboard of the bed.

Dirty could feel her cumming as he pushed in and out of her. Before he knew it, he released his load into his girl, and they both collapsed together. It took Midnight a minute to regain her composure, but when she did, she looked into her man's eyes.

"I love you, baby," Midnight whispered.

"I love you too," Dirty replied just as his phone started ringing again.

As Dirty took the call, Midnight got up and went to the bathroom. Looking at the number, Dirty was already thinking the worst.

"What up?" he answered, trying to sound like he was asleep.

"Wake up, young nigga. I may have some more business for you," Godzilla stated.

Dirty almost hung up the phone in the dopeboy's face. Instincts told him that he was being set up, but greed made him wanna hear the man out.

"What's the business?" Dirty asked. He just listened as Godzilla spoke about the robbery and carjacking that had happened the night before. His killer instincts were starting to kick in, and he was thinking that maybe they were trying to set him up.

"Was the nigga down with you?" Dirty asked.

"He get his work from us, but he ain't part of my crew," Godzilla explained.

Dirty knew right then not to say anything about the rims, but he would play along with the game. "Right now, I'm focused on the business I got with you because I don't want you putting these other wanna-bes in mines," he stated.

The comment made Godzilla laugh because he already knew what the young hitman was getting at. "Don't sweat that. I got my money on you," Godzilla said. "I just thought you may wanna make some extra bread," he continued.

"Shit, I'll think about it and get back to you," Dirty said. He needed to rest a little after the sexscapade he and Midnight had just had. He ended the call just as Midnight stepped back out of the bathroom.

"Is everything alright, baby?" she asked as she climbed back in the bed.

"Yep. That was just Godzilla calling with another job possibility," Dirty said. He explained how the man he'd robbed and carjacked was an associate of Godzilla, and the dude wanted to know who had the nerve to get at him. Midnight laughed at her man as she snuggled her naked body up against Dirty and listened to him talk until they both fell asleep.

***

To Krash's surprise, Keebler was already at the house when he woke up. As he sat outside in a black Impala, there was no doubt what his friend had on his mind. Before going to meet with Keebler to hear the game plan, he decided to make a pot of coffee for them to sip on while they talked business. While the coffee brewed, Krash put some powder in a dollar bill and broke it down. After taking two large piles up each nostril and catching the immediate drain, he was now awake and ready to grind.

Once the coffee was finished brewing, he poured two cups and went outside to meet his best friend.

"I'm surprised you up so early," Keebler said with a smile and a powder covered nose.

"I knew that since you didn't have Zya to keep you company overnight, you'd be up bright and early and ready to let off some steam," Krash replied as he passed one of the cups of coffee.

"I don't know how you know me so well, but you just hit the nail right on the head, nigga," Keebler said between sips of coffee.

"So, you ready to hit dude I had lined up out north?" Krash asked.

Keebler just nodded as a reply because he was snorting more powder. They discussed how they would pull off the robbery while continuing to get high and drink coffee for the next hour before heading out to the north side of town.

***

Out in North Memphis, Keebler could tell he was in the hood by the looks of the houses. For a person not from the city, a first glance at the area would have caused them to think there wasn't a lot of money being produced. However, in reality, one of the biggest drug dealers in the city not only had the area on lock, but he lived where he trapped. After being affiliated for years with one of the local gangs that was known for killing, this one dealer had gotten too comfortable with his hustle. Now, it was about to bite him in the ass.

"Check it, Keebler. The nigga Tank ain't just going to give up the bread without a fight," Krash admitted.

"You already know I love a challenge," Keebler replied as he maneuvered the stolen Impala through traffic.

"All I ask is that you wait until we get the shit before we knock the nigga's head off," Krash stated.

"I got you, homie. We get in, we take everybody hostage, then we go for the gold," Keebler repeated the plan.

Krash directed his friend how to get to the house through one of the many alleys throughout the area. When they pulled up behind the house, it was just as Krash said it would be. Both men carried two

Glock .23s with extra clips. They carefully cocked the guns to make sure a round was in the chamber. Both men then took four piles of powder up each nostril to get the motivation they both needed.

"Let's go get this paper," Krash said as he led the way toward the back door.

Without warning, Krash kicked in the back door, startling the people inside. On point, Keebler ran in with both Glocks aimed and Krash bringing up the rear. The door led to what looked like a den where three men were playing XBOX ONE on a huge flatscreen on the wall.

"You already know what this is. We want everything, and I don't like to repeat myself," Keebler demanded.

"Fuck y'all," one of the men said, trying to be tough. Instead of replying to the outburst, Keebler immediately shot the man in the head, instantly killing him.

Krash stepped up to the man who ran the traphouse. "Don't make us have to tear the place up, Tank. Give us the shit, and you won't become a victim of the shit," he told the man.

It took Tank a second to realize who actually had the nerve to run up in his spot.

"Just be cool, Krash," Tank pleaded with his hands in the air. He knew the men were serious because of the dead body beside him.

"Let's go, nigga!," Keebler impatiently.

Tank led the way to the bedroom. "There's a secret compartment in the closet. I got twenty bricks and fifty racks in it. You can have it all, my nigga. Just don't kill me please," Tank said, begging for his life.

Keebler stepped quietly up to his victim and put a fake smile on his face. "Very carefully, go get everything, and I'll be on my way," Keebler said slowly.

Tank did everything he asked, all while praying to make it out of the situation alive. He vowed to make both men pay, but he had something special for Krash who'd crossed him in the worst way. He was so wrapped up in his thoughts of revenge as he grabbed the work from the stash spot that he never saw Keebler step up behind him until it was too late.

Boc! Boc! Boc! Boc! Boc! Boc!

Six shots to the back of the head at point blank range left Tank's body slumped over in the closet. Keebler took the duffelbag from the lifeless body. He heard four more gunshots coming from the front of the house as he retraced his steps. Krash killed the only surviving victim so there wouldn't be anyone to point them out in the future. Without saying a word, they both stepped back out the back door and disappeared in the alley.

Keebler parked his car in the Country Apartments out in the Whitehaven area. He drove the Impala to a place he figured was safe to dump the car before setting it on fire. The two men casually walked to the front of the apartments where the Crown Vic was parked.

"It don't matter how many times I see this paint, it always makes you do a double take," Krash said as the hopped in the car.

"That's what that bowling ball blue paint do," Keebler stated proudly. As soon as he started the car, the sound system thumped hard in the trunk. When the hook came on, Keebler started singing to the beat.

"I got a gameplan; on how to come up from nothin'/

So, here's the plan, man; for all them niggas who frontin'/

We 'bout to shut 'em down; and make 'em break into somethin'/

Now you can try me, dog; you wanna see if I'm stuntin'"

"Who is that?" Krash asked while bouncing around in his seat.

"That's Flea shit! That nigga whole CD bumping," Keebler replied.

"You gotta make me a copy of that junt right there. He make a nigga hype," Krash said before pulling out the dollar bill he filled with powder. As they headed back to Krash's spot, they both listened to the music while swerving through traffic.

***

Out in North Memphis, Twin was doing what he did on a daily basis, and that was get money. Since it was not only the beginning of the month, but also the first day of the weekend, business was almost nonstop. He'd been doing so well that he was on his last ounce of crack cocaine before he realized he needed to re-up. At the rate business was going, there was no way he'd make it through the night before running out. He pulled out his cell phone and called his plug but got no answer. He tried calling three more times, only to get the voicemail, so he made up his mind that as soon as he got a chance to dip off he would.

Two neighborhoods over, Twin pulled up on the street his plug lived on and found it full of police cars. Because of the glossy silver paint on his two-door Cutlass and the huge 26-inch rims that made the car sit like a truck, all eyes were instantly on him. This left him no choice but to drive on so he wouldn't draw any more attention to himself.

As he got closer to the house, he realized all the police cars were at the plug's house. Twin shook his head, thinking the narcotics had hit the traphouse again, until he spotted the coroner's van parked in the driveway. Immediately fearing the worst, Twin pulled up to the curb and parked before jumping out. He was immediately met by a hustler named Ya-Yo, who was also a gang member associated with the same crew as Tank.

"What's going on?" Twin asked immediately. A lot of people had no clue that he was gang affiliated because he always moved behind the scenes.

"Somebody ran up in the spot and killed three people" Ya-Yo said.

"Was Tank one of them?" Twin cautiously asked. The watery eyes he saw when Ya-Yo looked at him said enough, but he still wanted a verbal response.

"Tank dead, bruh," Ya-Yo replied before he started crying.

The two men hugged each other for a moment then turned toward the house just as the coroners started bringing body bags out one by one. People openly mourned as they watched the coroner's van slowly pull away from the house.

Twin wanted some answers, so he went to the crowd of onlookers standing around and started asking questions. He couldn't believe that in the middle of the hood, in broad daylight, somebody had crept in and killed three people without being seen. Somebody knew something, and he would've stayed around all night until he found what he was looking for, but the detectives were now snooping around asking questions as well. The last thing on Twin's mind was talking to some police, so he casually eased to his car and dipped off undetected.

5

Hours later, Dirty was woken up by the sound of his phone ringing.

"Yeah," he answered sleepily on the third ring.

"Get up, young nigga. I got that package ready for you," the familiar voice said through the phone.

"Where you wanna meet at?" Dirty asked, already getting out the bed.

"How soon can you get to South Memphis?" the voice asked.

"Give me thirty minutes tops," Dirty replied.

"Hit me up when you in the area," the voice stated firmly before ending the call.

"Who was that?" Midnight asked as she woke up.

"Big bruh want us to meet up with him in South Memphis. He said he got that bread for me," Dirty explained.

At the mention of handling some business, Midnight was up for the day. Ten minutes later, they were in traffic headed to the south side.

***

Out in Coro Lake, Krash put the twenty bricks they'd just gotten from Tank in the attic.

"Leave a few of them out. I know a nigga who'll take some off our hands for a good price," Keebler explained while he separated the fifty thousand they had. Twenty thousand of it was going to Dirty, which left them with fifteen thousand dollars each.

"How many you want?" Krash asked from the attic.

"Just get three for now," his best friend replied.

Once they had everything situated, it was time to hit the streets. Krash said he felt like driving, so they both hopped in his Crown Vic and headed to South Memphis.

There was always some activity going on in South Memphis, and as Krash pulled up where Flea was known to hustle, it was no different. Traffic was naturally flowing nonstop when Krash pulled up. At first, Flea was nowhere to be seen. Then Keebler saw him hop out of a station wagon counting money.

"My nigga stay paper chasing," Keebler said with a smile.

Krash found a parking space up the street from the traphouse. Both men pulled out folded dollar bills that were stuffed with powder and took three piles up each nostril.

"Let's go stunt on these young niggas," Keebler said excitedly as they both made sure to clean their noses before hopping out the car. To their surprise, Flea was standing calmly at the trunk of the car waiting for his friends to get out.

"What it do, rich niggas?" Flea asked with his famous shiny smile.

"Close your mouth before you blind us, nigga," Krash said with a smile as they both greeted the young hustler.

"To what do I owe this pleasure?" Flea asked as he gave the men dap. "I know y'all ain't went through both of those zips already," he continued before they could answer.

"Shit, I still got more than half of mine left," Krash admitted.

"This visit is about us getting off some work," Keebler said.

"What y'all working with? You know we can get anything off around here," Flea boasted.

Just as Keebler was about get about business, Dirty came speeding down the street putting all the hustlers on alert, including Flea, who knew how he got down.

Nobody said anything, but as Keebler openly watched hustlers distance themselves from the action, he couldn't help but smile. Even Krash noticed how the vibe of the hood suddenly changed. Flea thought about walking off, but he also knew he hadn't showed Keebler and Krash anything but love, so he felt they wouldn't let anything bad happen to him. He looked Keebler in the eyes, trying to get a read on the man.

"You straight, Flea. He here to meet up with us," Keebler said upon reading his eyes.

Flea tried to relax, but when Dirty hopped out the car with his glock tucked openly in his waistline, he began to sweat. People up and down the street watched every move Dirty made as he stepped up to where his brothers were standing. He gave the men dap, including Flea, even though he didn't know him.

"What's the business?" Dirty asked, knowing all eyes were on him.

"Let me holler at you for a minute," Keebler said as he led the way back to the BMW. He already knew that Dirty always had Midnight with him, so instead of reaching for the front passenger door, he hopped in the backseat.

"What's up, lil sis?" Keebler spoke to Midnight as he passed the twenty grand to Dirty.

Without speaking, he started counting the money as Midnight indulged in a small conversation with Keebler. Just as he finished counting the money and passed it to his girl, his phone started ringing.

"What's up, cuz?" Dirty answered after recognizing the number. He listened as Twin spoke about his homeboys being killed and how he needed a quick plug on some work.

"How much work you trying to get?" Dirty asked.

The question immediately got Keebler's attention. He started to say something, but he didn't wanna seem like he was trying to listen to the conversation. Instead, he came up with an idea. Dirty let Twin know that he'd look around for some work, but everybody in the car knew what that meant. When he finally ended the call, he found Keebler watching him with a smile.

"What?" Dirty asked.

"I got what you looking for," Keebler replied. Right then, the young killer remembered Godzilla's robbery, thinking Keebler was trying to get off some of the work.

"You'll fuck with my kinfolks?" Dirty asked.

"Follow me to the Crown Vic," Keebler answered as he opened the door. He said his goodbyes to Midnight before hopping out the Beamer to find he was being watched.

"Boy, you sure know how to get niggas' attention," Keebler told Dirty as they stepped back up to where Krash and Flea were standing.

"Who got some weed out here?" Dirty asked suddenly.

"What you trying to get?" Flea spoke up. Even though he knew he was taking a chance dealing with Dirty, the hustler in him couldn't let any money get away.

"Get him an ounce of blueberry, and I got you," Keebler said.

As Flea dipped off to go get the weed, the three men casually stepped to the Crown Victoria.

"I got a brick here. Tell your cousin, since he family, just give me fifteen for the whole chicken," Keebler said as he pulled out one of the kilos of cocaine they took from Tank.

"Say no more," Dirty replied as he cuffed the drugs.

A minute later, Flea casually strutted back over to the group and gave a brown paper bag to Dirty. "That's on the house. Just come through and spend with me. They call me Flea," he said.

"I appreciate that, and I will be fucking with you," Dirty replied. "Shit, I'll be back through here later on today. I just need to get rid of these 26s I got," he continued.

"What you want for them?" Flea asked.

Both Keebler and Krash were surprised about how well the two youngsters were getting along. Flea and Dirty made a deal to get up with each other later and exchanged numbers before Dirty hopped back in the car and sped off.

"I see you made a new friend," Keebler said with a smile, all the while noticing other hustlers stepping back out on the grind.

"I'd rather have a nigga like that on my side than as an enemy," Flea replied honestly.

The comment made the men laugh because it was true. Although Flea had only heard stories of how Dirty got down in the streets, Keebler and Krash knew firsthand because he was part of their family.

Out of the blue, Flea started eyeing Krash's car with a smile on his face.

"What's so funny, young nigga?" Krash asked.

"I think I'm gone get me one of these," Flea answered. He already knew what color he wanted and everything. Since his order was coming through later in the day on the rim tip, he figured it was time he stepped up his game.

"I got a couple of bricks I need to get off. We got good prices on deck if you know anyone looking for a steal," Keebler said suddenly. The look Flea gave him said everything that needed to be said, so they strutted up the street to where the other hustlers were.

***

Once Dirty was safely back in traffic, he called his cousin back up.

"For you to be calling me back so quick, I know you got some good news for me," Twin said when he answered the call.

"Where you at now?" Dirty asked.

"I just got back to the block, and I'm money sick because I'm missing out on this come up," Twin replied miserably.

The comment made Dirty laugh. "Just be cool, nigga. I'll be at you in less than ten minutes. Just make sure you got fifteen racks on deck," he said and ended the call before Twin could answer.

Just as Dirty said, minutes later, he was pulling up at the traphouse Twin ran. Before he was out of the car good, Twin was at the car.

"Please tell me you got some work with you," he asked.

"My nigga gave me this to give you and said that since you like family, just give him fifteen for it," Dirty said before pulling out the kilo of cocaine. Twin immediately eyed the wrapping, recognizing the logo.

"It's real dope, cuz," Dirty spoke. He saw the look on his cousin's face and thought he didn't believe it was real dope. He didn't know that the kilo in his possession came from the same person Twin got his work from.

"You think you can plug me in with your boy?" Twin asked, already thinking of payback for the death of his homeboys.

"Just let me know when you ready," Dirty replied. "As for now, I need that fifteen if you trying to get about your paper," he continued.

Twin pulled a wad of one-hundred-dollar bills out of his pocket and gave it to his cousin. Dirty carefully counted out the money before putting the drugs in his cousin's possession. Once the transaction was complete, Twin made an excuse to get about his business.

Before Dirty was around the corner good, Twin was on his phone.

"What's up, bruh?" the voice he was looking for answered.

"I may have found who killed Tank," Twin said. He explained to Ya-Yo that his cousin had just dropped off a brick of cocaine with Tank's logo on it.

"You think your cousin had something to do with it?" Ya-Yo asked. The thought had never crossed Twin's mind before. As he thought about it, he knew in his heart that Dirty was just a middleman. His cousin killed for a living, but if he'd been a part of the robbery, he would've admitted as much.

"I'm going to get to the bottom of this, but when I call and tell you it's time to push, be ready," Twin said with authority.

"I'm always ready to put in some work," Ya-Yo replied before ending the call.

Twin was in hustler mode, so he decided to clear his mind by getting money.

***

"So, now that we have the money, how are we going to deal with Godzilla?" Midnight asked as her man headed back to the eastside.

"I know of a vacant house on Brutonwood Cove. We'll get him there and kill him without anyone being able to identify us," Dirty explained.

In his mind, it would be simple. Get the victim to the fake traphouse and put in that work with his brothers. While it was on his mind, he headed to start getting the ball rolling. He called Godzilla on his phone and got an answer on the third ring.

"What's up, young nigga? You must have some good news for your boy if you up this early in the day," Godzilla said cheerfully. Dirty could tell he was in traffic from the sounds of music playing in the background.

"I need to meet up with you right quick. Where you at?" Dirty asked.

"I'm in traffic at the moment, but we can meet up wherever," Godzilla answered. Dirty gave him the place to be within the next hour and ended the call.

***

Out in South Memphis, Keebler and Krash were sitting back watching Flea and the other hustlers get about their money. The other two kilos had already been sold on consignment to a young hustler by the name of Big Dee. Since Flea spoke highly of the man, they decided to give him a chance. Now, as they watched the young hustler paper chase, it was apparent that the man knew how to get down. Flea had asked the men to stay and chill with him, but now they were getting antsy.

"You ready to roll out?" Keebler asked suddenly.

"I thought you would never ask," Krash said back.

They quickly hollered at Flea before making their way to the Crown Vic. After quickly getting situated, they pulled off knowing they were being watched.

***

Since Godzilla had an hour before he had to meet up with Dirty, he decided to go see his favorite cousin at work. Upon pulling up at the workplace, he could see they were busy at the moment and almost decided to leave, but it was too late. The person he was there to see had already spotted him, so he went on in the establishment.

"What's up, kinfolk?" the female voice greeted him cheerfully.

"What's good, Zya?" Godzilla greeted back as he stepped behind the counter like he worked at the gas station.

As Zya dealt with the customers, they held small conversation like they didn't have a care in the world. They had grown up together, were raised more like brother and sister, and were really close.

"I met a dude," Zya said suddenly once they were alone in the gas station.

"For real? When you gone let me meet him?" Godzilla asked.

***

Dirty decided to stop at the crib and pick up the rims he'd taken the night before. That way, after he finished with the meeting with Godzilla, he would take the money he got from his cousin to Keebler before going back to South Memphis. He pulled up at the meeting spot fifteen minutes early, hoping to find a good spot to post up and wait. To his surprise, he spotted the M6 Coupe already parked with smoke floating up through the moonroof. Godzilla was smoking on a blunt while nodding his head to the bass thumping hard in the trunk. Dirty slowly pulled up alongside him so his window was right at Godzilla's window. They both rolled down their windows with a smile.

***

Once Krash had safely made it back to his side of town, he started getting a bad vibe. Immediately, Godzilla came to mind.

"How are we going to deal with dude?" he asked.

"Lil bruh got a spot in the Sheffield area that we will make Godzilla's last resting spot," Keebler replied. "We gone already be inside posted when he get there and handle the business real quick and quietly," he continued.

Krash understood how they were supposed to handle the business. Something just didn't feel right to him, and he expressed his feelings. Keebler listened to his best friend, then reassured him that everything would be cool as long as they stuck to the script.

"Look, we gone handle this business tonight. Then tomorrow, we'll ride through South Memphis and hit Face and his crew," Keebler said. Hearing about the opportunity to make more money made Krash smile. Keebler's phone started ringing, interrupting their conversation. After looking at the number, he smiled.

"I gotta go meet up with Zya," Keebler said, already hopping out the car.

"Watch yourself and hit me up before it gets dark outside," Krash yelled after his friend as he strutted to the curb where his car was parked.

***

The meeting with Godzilla didn't take any time at all. Dirty sold the man a dream about how he'd found out that Keebler sold dope out of a traphouse in East Memphis. Godzilla got heated as he listened because the man who had robbed him was right under his nose the entire time, and niggas were claiming not to know him. Dirty promised to hit Godzilla up once he safely had the man in his sights, and that quickly put a smile on the killer's face. With an understanding established between them, the men both rolled up their windows as they

calmly pulled off.

63

6

Zya never got an answer when she called Keebler and thought she ran him off by not sleeping with him the night before. As much as she was feeling the man, if that was all he was interested in, then maybe it was best he went about his business. It had been an hour since she'd tried calling when she spotted the Crown Vic turning into the gas station. Without realizing it, she started smiling like a kid in a candy store, and that was the first thing Keebler noticed when he entered the building.

"I take it you're glad to see me," Keebler stated as he walked up to the counter. He didn't seem to notice, but he had a smile on his face as big as hers.

"The feeling must be mutual," Zya replied seductively as she gave him a light kiss on the lips.

They made small talk for the next thirty minutes while Zya did her job until she remembered the conversation she had with her cousin. Although she loved Godzilla like a brother, his reputation was known to run a man off once he found out they were related. She was really feeling Keebler, so the last thing Zya wanted was for him to leave and never come back. Eventually, the inevitable would happen, so she figured she'd try to get the meeting out of the way before her feelings got deeper for the man in front of her.

"I got somebody I want you to meet," Zya said hesitantly once the last customer left.

"Who is it?" Keebler asked while eyeing her.

He caught the hesitancy in her voice and thought she was afraid to tell him she had a child or two. That would've explained all that thickness she carried around proudly. He began envisioning her naked, and a huge smile popped onto his face. Zya saw the smile, already knowing he was thinking about her. She decided to tell him while the smile was there but regretted it the moment she said her cousin's name.

"My cousin Godzilla wanna meet you," Zya said and watched the smile completely vanish from his face. For a minute, Keebler just stared at Zya to see if she was playing, all the while trying to get his swagger back.

"Why do I need to meet him?" Keebler asked once he got his composure back. The tone in his voice spoke venom, but Zya didn't back down. She explained that they were first cousins who grew up together like brother and sister, and his opinion about her man meant a lot to her. Keebler just listened as she spoke, in disbelief of how bad his luck was. Knowing what his immediate future held, killing Godzilla became his top priority.

"I'm about to roll out, but I'll think about what you said," Keebler said as he made his way to the closest exit.

"Will I see you again?" Zya asked just as he touched the door. She was used to men walking out and never returning.

"You can bet your life on it," Keebler said and winked at her before walking out.

Before Keebler was sitting in his car good, he was already on the phone making a call.

"I know I said hit me up before it got dark, but I didn't mean this soon, homie," Krash's deep voice blared through the phone.

"Nigga, Zya is first cousins with Godzilla," Keebler said immediately. When the phone got quiet, he knew he had his best friend's attention, so he relayed the conversation they'd just had.

"Are you serious, nigga?" Krash asked after Keebler finished talking.

"I'm on my way to you now. We about to find this fool and squash him on the spot before this shit get out of hand," Keebler said in a tone that Krash was too familiar with.

"I'll be outside waiting," he assured him then ended the call to find his girl watching him closely. Immediately, that bad feeling came back to the surface.

Keebler went against everything he believed in and went looking for a car to steal in the daytime. He quickly hit some apartments and found some contenders, but nothing really suited what the mission called for until he pulled up at a shopping center on Raines Road in the Whitehaven area. A black Dodge Charger with a HEMI logo shining on its side was parked in a spot reserved for employees, so Keebler knew he had some time to work with before the car was even reported stolen. The fact that he was at a busy shopping center was his only problem. Keebler had to ease to the car and get in it without attracting too much attention to himself. Because the car had tinted windows, it was the perfect car to pull down on somebody in, and Keebler was determined to get it.

There was an auto parts store across the street from the shopping center, and that was where Keebler parked his car. He went into the parts store and quickly purchased a heavy-duty screwdriver and double padded mechanic gloves. Instead of going back to his car, Keebler casually headed across the street to the shopping center while putting the gloves on. Seeing his target, he eased up to the driver's side door and pulled on the door handle. To his surprise, not only was the door unlocked, but there was no alarm on the car.

"Today must be my day," Keebler told himself as he closed the door so nobody could see him under the tint playing with wires. A minute later, the Charger came to life, and Keebler sped away from the scene.

***

Since Krash already knew what kind of mission they were about to go on, he quickly got dressed in all black and loaded up two AK-47s with a hundred round drum on each. He glanced back at his girl Trina just as he was about to head out on the porch to wait for Keebler and found her with tears in her eyes. She knew how the men got down, so whenever rifles were brought out, she knew murder was in the air, and she was scared for her man. Krash carefully set the rifles down and walked over to her.

"Everything is going to be alright, baby," Krash whispered in that deep voice that drove Trina crazy.

"Just make it back home to me," she pleaded just as he knelt down to kiss her soft lips. The sweet scent of her body fragrance made Krash wanna fuck her brains out right then and there, but he knew his best friend needed him. He made the promise, then went outside to load the choppers in his car. Just as he got seated behind the wheel, the roaring of a monster engine could be heard in the distance.

Before Keebler even made it to the driveway, Krash could see him bouncing around behind the wheel. The men made eye contact, and that was all that needed to be said. Krash pulled off in his Crown Vic, following closely behind the Charger to keep the license plate hidden. He did want to know where Keebler found that powerful car, though, so he called his best friend.

"Please tell me you calling to give your boy some white girl," Keebler answered the call.

"I called to find out where you found that beast at, but you know I got you," Krash replied with a laugh. They held a quick conversation while they found a safe place to pull over. Without looking too obvious, Krash parked beside the Charger to transfer the choppers without people seeing what they were doing.

"It's that golden time of day, nigga," Keebler said, quoting a Frankie Beverly featuring Maze song. Without a word, Krash passed a twenty-dollar bill filled with cocaine to his friend before getting back in his own car. Seconds later, both vehicles were back in traffic.

***

With nothing to do, Godzilla smiled when he got a phone call from his boss.

"Shorty Bud! What it do?" Godzilla answered happily.

"I need to meet up with you A. S. A. P.," Shorty Bud said firmly. Without waiting for a reply, the young king pen kept talking. "I'm about to ride up to the courts and do some gambling. You big money. Come try your luck," Shorty Bud said jokingly.

"I'm on my way," Godzilla said and ended the call. He was nervous about the untimely meeting, but he figured it couldn't have been too bad if he wanted to meet in public. The courts they were meeting at were at Halle Stadium next to the Mount Moriah police precinct. Because the meeting was at a known court right next to the police station, the man was at ease as he headed in that direction.

Keebler led the way to I-240 and headed east with Krash following closely behind to hide his tags and prevent him from being pulled over. As he pushed the Charger almost to its limits, he wasn't surprised to see his best friend keeping up. They both had motors that surpassed what the police had under the hood, so he knew Krash's car was able to keep up with the HEMI. They took the interstate all the way to the Highway 385 junction, only to hop off at the Ridgeway exit. As they were on the backside of the hood, Keebler led the way to the Fox Apartments where they parked the Crown Vic. Before Krash had the door closed good, Keebler was speeding back out of the apartments.

"How we gone find this nigga?" Krash asked as they sped up Mount Moriah like the street belonged to them.

"First, we hit all known hot spots in the area. If he don't turn up, we check traphouses," Keebler explained. "We just gotta find this nigga, and now," he continued as they headed toward the courts.

As they sped past the police station on their way to the nearest community center, Krash glanced over at the crowded basketball courts, and something caught his attention.

"Whoa! Whoa! Turn around and pull up at that court," Krash demanded as he turned all the way around in his seat, trying to see if he really saw what he thought he'd seen.

"This ain't the time to catch a nigga up. We gotta stay focused," Keebler said as they were passing over the interstate.

"What if it's the Godzilla nigga?" Krash asked, all the time smiling.

In response, Keebler bogarded traffic as he sharply turned the wheel, making the Charger do a 180-degree turn as the rear tires screeched and oncoming traffic stopped to prevent causing a wreck. By the time the smoke cleared enough for traffic to resume, Keebler was in the turning lane, about to pull up at the basketball courts.

"What I'll do is ride around one time just to see how many exits we have to work with," Keebler said as he slowly pulled up on the lot.

"This is the only way in and out," Krash said matter-of-factly. He'd shot ball at this court on numerous occasions, so he was already familiar with the area. "The only way we can do this is to pull up, jump out, and clear shit out. Then we'll have to buck traffic to get away because the cops will be coming," Krash explained, hoping his friend would think twice about what they were about to do.

"Fuck it! Let's do this," Keebler said before he turned around. As they headed back toward their target, both men held a chopper in their laps.

They found Godzilla talking to several men by his car, one of them being Shorty Bud. After pulling up a few spaces from where the money green BMW was parked with the system blasting, Keebler quickly threw the car in Park. Both men jumped out with choppers in hand and immediately sprang into action.

Boc! Boc! Boc! Boc! Boc! Boc! Boc! Boc! Boc! Boc! Boc! Boc! Boc!

The continuous rapid fire sent everybody outside scrambling to find cover, though most of them were unsuccessful. The ceaseless gunfire went on for what seemed like forever before sudden silence filled the park. Both men quickly hopped back inside the Charger, and Keebler sped off into traffic as police officers ran out of the neighboring police station to see what was happening. The only thing they saw was a black souped-up vehicle speeding up Mount Moriah on the wrong side of traffic.

As Keebler sped back into the Fox Apartments, he made sure to watch the rearview mirror. When nobody turned in behind them, he headed to the Crown Vic.

"By the time you get situated, I'll be walking back toward you," Keebler said as Krash hopped out while trying to hide both choppers as best as he could. Before another word was said, the Charger sped off toward the back of the apartments. After finding a deserted spot, Keebler quickly wiped down as much of the car as he could with his shirt before setting the shirt on fire and dropping it in the driver's seat of the car. Without being noticed, he casually strutted toward the sound of a system in the distance. By the time he was two streets away from the vehicle that was now fully engulfed in flames, Krash was pulling down on his friend to pick him up. Once he was safely inside the car, they cruised toward the nearest exit.

Back at the courts, the police presence was thick as they tried to piece together what had just happened just yards away from the station. As far as they knew, eight people were dead on the scene, and the total number of injured people was still unclear. Unfortunately, both Godzilla and Shorty Bud were amongst the deceased. Along with them were two members of the Black Gorilla Cartel who were visiting from Miami, Florida. The men were in town to discuss a new price for the weight Shorty Bud was buying and ended up being caught in the crossfire of a battle that wasn't theirs to fight.

7

It was a good thing the interstate was right down the street from the Fox Apartments because as soon as Krash pulled out on Mount Moriah, the first thing they noticed was the heavy police presence.

"Get out of this area now," Keebler instructed nervously. The last thing they needed was to get pulled over with two choppers that were just used in a massacre next door to a police station in the back seat.

"What do you think I'm trying to do?" Krash replied as he pulled into the turning lane. The light was red, so they waited with the other vehicles, all the while looking at the entrance ramp leading to the interstate.

The sound of Keebler's phone ringing made both men flinch. Recognizing the number, he answered on the second ring.

"Where you at, big bruh?" Dirty asked.

"In traffic at the moment. What's up?" Keebler said. He wanted to see where the young killer's mind was.

"I got that bread for you. I'm on my way back out south now and wanted to know if you could meet me out there," the hitman asked.

He could sense that something wasn't right from the way Keebler answered the phone.

"Give me a few minutes to get to you," Keebler said just as they safely jumped on the interstate and were now blending in with traffic. Dirty agreed and was about to hang up, but Keebler stopped him.

"Flea is a real nigga, and we see him as part of the family. Spare my lil' dude," he stated firmly. For a minute, all he heard was laughter.

"I like Flea. I don't have many friends, but trust me when I say he's in good hands," Dirty said once he finished laughing.

"Just like Allstate. See you in a minute," Keebler said and ended the call. He sat back and relaxed the rest of the ride back to Whitehaven.

***

Flea was still outside getting about his hustle when he noticed the black BMW turn onto the street. Just as they had done earlier in the day, hustlers began to ease away from the block once they figured out whose car it was. As bad as he wanted to dip off himself, he knew he was the reason Dirty was back in the hood. The last thing he wanted to do was look like he was avoiding Dirty and put a target on his back. He sucked in a deep breath, then stepped out to the curb so he was clearly seen as he watched the Beamer stop in front of him.

"I told you I'd be back through to fuck with you," Dirty hopped out the car saying. The imprint on the front of his shirt let anybody who was out watching know that he was strapped. He casually stepped around to the back passenger side door and opened it.

"Damn! Them junts is hard," Flea said as he stepped up to get a better look. He carefully pulled a rim out to get an idea of how he would stunt on the town. Flea's mind was made up that the rims were his. He pulled out a wad of money and passed it to Dirty.

"Is this the amount we agreed on?" Dirty asked in his business tone.

"The last thing I want is a problem with you. I can wait for you to count it if you want," Flea replied with his hands up. Dirty waved the thought off with a smile and put the money in his pocket. As they began pulling the other three rims out the car, a junkie Flea knew came walking up the street.

Word traveled fast when a mass shooting happened next to a police station. The fact that Shorty Bud and Godzilla were among the dead made the news top priority in the gossip world. Because it was hard to believe the notorious Shorty Bud had gotten caught slipping with his top enforcer, people drove to the courts to see if the rumors were true for themselves. Police had to shut down Mount Moriah while they investigated the murders to keep people from interfering with the investigation, and they still had a hard time. With over fifty shells at the crime scene and witnesses placing two shooters at the scene, all the authorities could tell was that someone had a personal vendetta against one of the dead.

While Dirty stood out talking to Flea, Midnight sat calmly in the car playing with her phone. This was exactly what she was doing when a breaking news alert popped up on one of her apps. She liked to keep up with the news chatter, especially since they were the cause of a lot of it. This way, they stayed one step ahead of law enforcement at all times. She clicked on the app to see what was so important but wasn't prepared for what she was now looking at.

"Baby! Check this out," Midnight half-yelled as she stepped out the car.

Flea was startled when the door flew open suddenly, but he would have sworn his heart stopped beating for a full sixty seconds as he stared at the most beautiful female he'd ever laid eyes on. He knew he had to keep his composure in front of Dirty, so he quickly regained his swagger. As Midnight passed her man the phone, she glanced over at Flea, noticing him for the first time. They made eye contact, and Midnight almost dropped the phone. The persona that the dopeboy had was known to lure in some of the most unexpecting types of female, and this day was no different. It was already understood that he wanted her. Now, he'd seen it in her eyes that she wanted him just as bad.

"What the fuck?" Dirty said, snapping the two from their hypnotic trance.

Midnight thought she'd gotten caught trying to seduce Flea with her stare and was about to say something until Dirty spoke up again.

"Somebody killed Shorty Bud and Godzilla," he said while thinking about the twenty grand he had. He couldn't have cared less about the men being dead. He knew once Keebler found out, he'd have to give the money back. He started to think about the conversation they had last and the way Keebler sounded. Could his big brother have pulled that off in broad daylight? Dirty asked himself. He was about to find out soon enough because Keebler came swerving around the corner with the system bumping Yo Gotti at that moment.

The whole ride back to Whitehaven, Krash was quiet and focused on the road. He hopped off the interstate at the Millbranch exit, then laughed.

"That was some scary shit," Krash said as he exhaled.

"It was, but it had to be done," Keebler admitted. He told his best friend where he'd parked his car, then trailed him to the Coro Lake suburbs just to make sure everything was good.

"What you about to get into?" Keebler asked once they were safely at the house. Krash then explained that his girl was scared earlier and that he wanted to spend the rest of the day with her to ease her mind.

"That's understandable," Keebler said while feeling kind of bad about the situation. "Let sis know that the business had to be handled. I'm about to ride out south to make sure Dirty don't kill Flea. Holler at me if you need anything," he continued. Krash watched as his best friend got in his car and sped off like nothing had just happened before getting the choppers out the car to dispose of in the lake.

Keebler spotted the black BMW parked at the curb and pulled up behind it.

"What are you young niggas up to?" he asked as he stepped up to where they stood. While the men were occupied, Midnight quickly retreated back to the safety of the tinted-out Beamer.

"You already know my daily ritual," Flea said and pulled out a wad of money so big that it barely folded.

"You niggas doing the thing, ain't it?" Keebler asked while smiling at how close the two had gotten.

"I got something for you," Dirty said suddenly. He reached in his pocket and started counting out money until Keebler stopped him.

"What you doing?" he asked.

"You must ain't heard the news yet?" Dirty asked. He was about to explain about the breaking news report that had popped up but got a surprise testimony.

"I know all about what you thinking about," Keebler stated, but the look in his eyes said everything. "Just hold on to that twenty because I got a job for you," he continued as Dirty counted the fifteen grand he'd gotten from his cousin for the brick of cocaine.

"I hope you keep it coming because my main dude is done," Dirty said with a smile. In a way, he was mad that he hadn't been there to see Godzilla get gunned down.

"What you about to get into?" Flea asked Keebler.

"Shit, my day clear as of now," he replied.

Flea explained how he'd just copped some rims and wanted to put them on something. "It's about time I do a little shining myself," he said.

Keebler agreed to take the hustler around town to find a ride, but he had to place his order with Dirty first.

"I got a address for you," Keebler said, then led the way to the car. He explained that he wanted a hit put on Calvin, and he wanted someone to thoroughly search the house and take all the dope and money inside. "You keep whatever money you get. Just bring me all the dope," Keebler bargained.

Dirty took the address and agreed to the deal. He already knew who Calvin was and who he worked for, so everybody was about to come up in the game. Dirty hopped in his car and sped off with Keebler and Flea pulling off only minutes after him to go car shopping.

***

Word had already gotten back to Zya about her cousin being killed, and she was about to lose her mind. She still had three hours left on her shift, and with nobody around to cover her, if she left the store unattended, there would be no job to come back to. As much as she wanted to call Keebler, his reaction to hearing they were kinfolks told her the man would show a lack of condolences. There was only one person she knew of who could fill her in on the real business, so she dialed his number.

"What's up, Zya?" Calvin answered on the second ring. She knew the rumors were true from the sound of Calvin's voice, but she still needed verbal confirmation.

"Is it true?" Zya asked hesitantly.

"It is," Calvin replied before breaking down, which caused Zya to cry herself.

For a moment, the two just cried, both missing someone close to them. Zya was first to regain her composure because a customer walked in.

"Are you alright, shorty?" the man asked, concerned. Zya nodded while giving him a smile, so he paid for his gas and left just as fast as he came.

"What happened?" Zya asked suddenly.

"Right now, all I know is they were ambushed at the basketball courts," Calvin replied once he got himself together. "We went to the scene, and it was fucked up. Somebody had a personal beef with them, but we going to find out who did it," he continued. Zya was about to plead to the man to just let it go but never got the chance. There was a loud thumping noise in the phone, followed by three gunshots before the phone went dead.

***

"Niggas round my way, they don't play, talk shit and get'cha issue/
They gone hit'cha wit some shit that make ya momma go and miss ya/
If they find you, they gone find ya sprinkled up, like a cupcake/
Holes to da dome so they won't recognize you at the wake/
Bosshog livin', ain't no slippin' when you in dem streets/
Get it how I live, I'm da truth, so I play for keeps/
Rollin' by the code, loose lips sink ships/
I'll never put my trust, in a nigga or a bitch."

"Young nigga, you going platinum with that shit," Keebler yelled to Flea over the system as he just smiled in return.

The bass was thumping so hard that it was a wonder that he was even heard. They had a blunt of Hydro being passed back and forth, and it had them both feeling good. The original plan was to go look for a car, but they'd ended up riding around flexing for an hour. When Flea suggested that Keebler turn down the music, it was then time to actually go car hunting.

"I want one of these," Flea said while rubbing on the soft leather seats.

"I know a lot that specializes in Crown Vics," Keebler said. "You won't be running quite like this, but we can get to that later on," he continued.

"Just find me a Vic," Flea said with a laugh. Keebler nodded then unmuted the music so he could start back flexing.

***

After leaving South Memphis, Midnight needed to take a long cold shower.

"What're you about to get into," she asked Dirty.

"Keebler put me on a serious lick. I was thinking about going to handle that now while we in traffic," Dirty answered.

"I wanna go home, so drop me off before you do anything else," Midnight demanded.

Dirty glanced over at his girl, about to make an issue about her aggression toward him, but he decided against it. He had money on his mind, and unless he directed the anger building up inside him toward getting about his hustle, he knew he'd slip up some kind of way and get caught up by the police. They both kept quiet, and the more Dirty drove in silence, the madder he was getting. He zig-zagged the Beamer through traffic to get to their house.

When he finally made it home, instead of pulling in the driveway, Dirty parked at the curb. Midnight glared at him before getting out the car. Dirty sped off, not even waiting to see if she made it in the house safely.

By the time Dirty was blended back in the afternoon traffic, his target's address was typed into the GPS. The deal Keebler made with him was now playing over in his head.

"It shouldn't be too hard to knock this nigga off by myself," he said to himself.

It would have definitely been a lot easier having Midnight at his side, but that wasn't the case this time. She had an attitude with him for some reason, and he vowed to find out why as soon as he got back home. At the moment, money and murder were on his mind, and it was a good thing because he was turning on the street of his mission.

In the driveway was only one car, and it was the black Cadillac that belonged to Calvin. The house looked quiet, which was understandable since his boys had just been killed.

"Well, might as well send you to join your boys," Dirty said before cocking his pistol to make sure a round was in the chamber. He parked on the curb a few houses down and hopped out. Without missing a beat, Dirty ran up to the house and kicked the front door off the hinges with one good kick. To his surprise, the target was sitting in the front room on the phone.

Boc! Boc! Boc!

All three shots caught their mark, killing Calvin instantly.

Dirty didn't really know what he was looking for at the time, but he immediately ran toward the bedrooms to begin searching. In the first bedroom were four bricks of what looked like cocaine sitting on a table. Beside them were stacks of money, and the hitman figured it was the day's earnings.

"You won't need this," Dirty said out loud, then laughed at his own joke. He found a huge duffelbag and put everything in it. He quickly went to search the second room, but it was just a normal bedroom. He was starting to think he'd gotten everything until he opened the back bedroom door.

"Shit," Dirty said while looking at a custom security system. As he stared at the monitors, he now knew how Keebler had slipped up. He quickly deleted recordings for the entire day and turned the security system off. He went to the closet and opened it up.

"Jackpot!" Dirty exclaimed.

***

The car lot Keebler took Flea to had some of everything.

"Shit! You can leave me here if you want. I know I'll be pulling off in something nice," Flea said as they got out the car. A car salesman spotted the customized Crown Vic when it pulled up on the lot and knew that was a future commission. Now, as the old man quickly stepped toward them, he spotted the shiny gold teeth in one man's mouth and knew he'd hit the jackpot.

"How may I help you gentlemen today?" the salesman asked with his biggest smile before Keebler could reply to his friend.

"I'm trying to ride off the lot in something nice," Flea said, getting straight to the point.

Keebler's phone started ringing. He looked at the screen and saw it was Zya.

"What's up, baby?" he answered on the second ring.

"Are you busy?" she asked in a shaky voice. Keebler knew then that she'd heard about her cousin being killed.

"I'm at the car lot with my nigga, but I'm never too busy for you," Keebler said cockily.

When Zya started crying through the phone, it was more than he could stand. Remembering what Flea had said about leaving him there, he decided to take him up on his offer.

"I need to go handle something, homie. If you need anything, just hit me up," Keebler told Flea, then rushed to the car when the young hustler nodded back.

***

In the closet were twenty more kilos and an open safe that had stacks of money in it. Dirty quickly put everything in the duffelbag, ready to get out the house. He did a once over in every room to make sure he'd grabbed everything, then eased out the front door. It had been ten minutes since he'd killed Calvin, so Dirty knew the police hadn't been called. He peeked out the front door to make sure no nosey neighbors were out before easing out the door. Just as he made it to the car, another vehicle came speeding down the street. Dirty put the duffelbag in the trunk and put in another clip in case he had to shoot his way out of the neighborhood. To his relief, the speeding car flew on by him without a second glance. It was time to get out of there, and Dirty

knew this much, so he jumped in the Beamer and pulled off.

8

Out in Coro Lake, Krash had gotten rid of both choppers and was now taking a long hot shower. Just as he was rinsing off his back, Trina seductively stepped in the shower. For a minute, they both just stood there eyeing each other down until the steam from the shower made it hard to see. Trina then reached out and firmly grabbed her man's nine-inch pipe. She slowly stroked him as she dropped down to her knees and prepared to put as much of him as she could take in her mouth. Krash, already knowing what to expect, just held on and prepared for the ride. Trina kissed the head of his wand, then proceeded to put it in her mouth.

"Shit!" Krash moaned as he slowly began fucking her mouth.

The more he grinded, the more she took down her throat. It never took long for him to reach ecstasy when Trina put her head game to use, and this time was no different. She was squeezing his balls with one hand while sucking on his dick and jerking him off with the other. Krash was so into it that he grabbed Trina by her hair and fucked her mouth like it was the last time he would ever feel himself inside her.

Before he knew it, his cream was shooting down her throat as he held her head to make sure she got every last drop.

Without missing a beat, Trina stood up and jumped in her man's arms. She knew Krash would catch her, and he did this time, allowing her to wrap her legs around his waist and slide down on his pipe.

"Oh! Baby!" Trina cooed in his ear as she fought to take every inch of her man.

Krash pumped in and out of her wetness very slowly, trying to open her up. Before they knew it, the sounds of moaning were all that could be heard as Trina took control. She rode her man, matching his every stroke with a stroke of her own.

"I love you baby," Trina whispered in his ear.

"I love you too," Krash said back.

He knew Trina was about to cum, so he spread her butt cheeks apart while leaning her against the wall. He began pounding her pussy fast and hard, making it talk to him.

"I'm cumming! I'm cum-ming!" Trina said as she bit down on her bottom lip. They both reached an orgasm at the same time, almost passing out in the hot shower. It took a moment to get their strength back, but when they did, they quickly washed each other up, then went to bed buck naked.

***

For some reason, hearing Zya crying on the phone hit a soft spot in Keebler, even though he was behind the pain she was feeling. The only thing on his mind was stopping her from hurting any more, but he had no clue how that would be done.

Halfway to the gas station, the phone started ringing, and Keebler was tempted to ignore it until he saw what number it was.

"What's good?" he answered on the third ring.

"Boy, did you put your lil brother on this time!" Dirty said cheerfully. "I know we had an original agreement, but after the love you showed me, big bruh, I gotta put you on," he continued.

"Where you at now?" Keebler asked. He was surprised to see that Dirty had dealt with Calvin so quickly, but he wasn't mad. Now that he had all his loose ends tightly tied up, he could strictly focus on hustling off the work he got.

"I'm still in the area, but I can be anywhere you need me to be in no time," Dirty replied. Keebler told him to go to the gas station and wait for him. "I'll be pulling up in a few minutes," Dirty said and ended the call.

Zya was busy with a customer when she spotted the black BMW pull up at a gas pump. Since she knew that Keebler was on his way to her, it automatically dawned on her that he was there waiting on her.

The fact that the driver of the Beamer never got out the car only confirmed what she was thinking. Minutes later, the familiar vibration of bass could be felt, letting Zya and Dirty know that Keebler was in the vicinity. She watched as the Crown Vic parked at the pump behind the BMW, and as sad as she was, a huge smile spread across her face. It was at that moment that she realized she was falling in love with Keebler.

From the size of the duffelbag Dirty pulled out the trunk, it was understood that he'd actually come up. Anyone could tell it was stuffed from the way he carried it to the car.

"What you got in there, a dead body?" Keebler asked as Dirty climbed in the passenger seat. Instead of replying, the hired killer just opened the duffelbag and watched Keebler as he stared at its contents in amazement.

"You got this from the crib?" he asked while thinking back to the day he'd robbed Calvin.

"Dude had a safe in the back bedroom, and the bricks were stacked next to it," Dirty explained.

"So, what kind of deal you wanna make now?" Keebler asked, strictly in hustler mode.

"I know what you said about me keeping the money, but I wouldn't have it if it wasn't for you," Dirty said. "You can keep all the work and half the money. Just promise me that I'm on the team when you take over the dope game. Whenever you got beef, I get the job," he continued.

Keebler acted like he was thinking about the proposition, but in his mind, the deal was already done. "Deal," Keebler said with a smile.

Inside the store, Zya was wondering what kind of business they were handling. She knew it was business because of the duffelbag she'd seen the young boy get out the trunk. She tried being patient, but her nosiness was getting the best of her, so she called Keebler.

"Your ears must be ringing because I was just about to call you," Keebler answered on the first ring.

"I bet you was. Are you going to sit in that car until I get off or come keep me company?" Zya asked.

"I actually need to dip off for a minute with my brother to handle some business," Keebler said. Zya immediately started whining, thinking he would leave and not come back. "I'm coming back, boo. We leaving the BMW here, so keep an eye on it," Keebler said as he started up his car.

Knowing one of the cars was staying here was all the consolation Zya needed. He had to bring the owner of the BMW back, and she'd be waiting when he did. She let them go handle their business while she got back to work.

***

Out in North Memphis, Twin was getting about his money, but his mind wasn't focused on the hustle. He kept thinking about his homeboy Tank being gunned down earlier in the day. Then his mind wandered to his cousin popping up with a kilo of dope with Tank's logo on it, even though he wasn't a dopeboy. Something wasn't right, and as he thought of the question his brother Ya-Yo had asked, he knew that although there was more money to be made, Twin had to get down to business. He dialed numbers on his phone as he headed to his car.

"Ya-Yo, be outside in a few minutes. We about to holler at my cousin's plug," Twin said as soon as Ya-Yo answered.

"I'll be on the block waiting," Ya-Yo replied. He was ready to put in some work, especially if it involved avenging the death of one of theirs. Twin immediately called Dirty next.

"What's up, cousin?" Dirty answered.

"I need to get up with your guy," Twin said, trying to sound business-like.

"You ate that chicken already?" Dirty asked in disbelief. He knew his cousin Twin was a real dopeboy, but that was the first time he'd known anyone to swang a kilo in less than a day.

"Business is always good in my hood. That's why I do this," Twin boasted. He heard Dirty speaking to someone and figured it was the person he'd gotten the work from earlier. It was starting to look more and more like Dirty had something to do with the murders.

"My guy said if you can meet us in the east, then come holler at him," Dirty said moments later.

"Bet that," Twin said a little too fast, but his cousin never caught the eagerness in his voice.

They agreed to a public meeting spot because Keebler didn't know what to expect. They were at The Memphis Inn, a small but affordable motel not too far from where Zya worked. It was a place where they could count the money from the lick Dirty made.

"I can't believe this," Dirty said after they'd finished counting and splitting the money.

"One hundred thousand is a nice pay day," Keebler said as he gave his young killer fifty grand while putting his half back in the duffelbag with the 25 bricks of pure cocaine. Keebler put the duffelbag in the trunk of his car behind the huge speakers so it couldn't be seen if anyone looked inside.

"Let's go meet my cousin before you take me to the car," Dirty suggested as they were pulling out into the almost nighttime traffic. Truth be told, the young killer was enjoying kicking it with Keebler and wasn't ready to end his day just yet.

***

Just as Twin was ending the phone call with his cousin, he was pulling up in the hood where Ya-Yo was known to hang. Ya-Yo, a man of his word, was standing out waiting patiently. From the bulge under his shirt, it was understood that he was ready for war.

"What's the business, bruh?" Ya-Yo asked as he hopped in the Cutlass and shook up with Twin.

"We about to ride out east to holler at the dude my cousin said he got that brick from," Twin explained. "I want you to see if you know this cat from the area while I lay the charm to find out what kind of nigga we dealing with," he continued.

"That's what's up, but are we whacking the nigga?" Ya-Yo asked. He was ready to put in some work, and in his mind, both Dirty and Keebler were guilty.

Twin knew why Ya-Yo was so eager to kill somebody. A lot of their homeboys claimed he didn't have the heart to be down, so this, in his mind, was the way to prove himself and possibly move up in the ranks.

Twin, on the other hand, couldn't have cared less about having rank. He was a dopeboy first and a gangster second. That was one of the reasons why Tank always showed him love, and for that reason, putting in some work was something Twin was looking forward to. There was still a script that had to be kept, and during the entire ride to the east side, he made sure Ya-Yo understood the real plan. Once he was sure his homeboy would stick to the script, he turned up the sound of his new system that he'd bought from Dirty. Since he was familiar with where they were going, it didn't take any time to get to the meeting spot, especially since it was just off the interstate on Perkins Road.

Once off the interstate, it dawned on Twin that he didn't know what vehicle to be looking for. As he pulled up on the shopping center lot, he headed toward Marshall's.

"Look around for a black BMW," Twin told Ya-Yo. He figured his cousin would be in his own car, but the Beamer was nowhere to be found.

"I don't see no BMW, but I think it's kinda odd that Crown Vic is parked by itself," Ya-Yo said, noticing how clean the car was. Twin stopped and stared at the car, trying to peer through the blacked-out tinted windows.

The Cutlass had been first spotted by Keebler as it pulled up on the lot. The silver paint shined off the clear coat, and although there was no argument which vehicle was cleanest, the way the two-door Cutlass sat up on the 26-inch wheels would make anyone do a double take. Dirty was just finishing rolling a blunt when Keebler got his attention.

"That's my cousin right there," Dirty said as he lit the Hydro blunt. Keebler automatically knew who the weed was from because it was the only weed he smoked. They sat in the car getting high for a minute before it dawned on Dirty that his cousin didn't know what they were riding in.

"Let me call this fool and let him know what we in," he said between coughs. He passed the weed back to Keebler as he called his cousin.

"Where you at, cuz?" Twin answered on the second ring.

"We sitting in the Crown Vic," Dirty replied as he rolled his window down and waved.

"I see y'all doing it big," Twin said as he cruised toward them.

Since Twin had no idea who was driving the Crown Vic, he decided to park so his window was next to his cousin. He ended the call just as his driver's side window rolled down. Both men in the Cutlass eyed Keebler to see if they'd seen him before but hadn't. Twin was now starting to think maybe it was just a coincidence that his cousin ended up with a package with his now deceased homeboy's logo on it.

"That shit smell good as a motherfucker, kinfolk! Let us hit that blunt," Twin said, mesmerized by the smell of the Hydro.

"How about you roll yourself one up while you and my nigga discuss business?" Dirty said before passing his cousin two big buds and a green leaf Optimo cigar.

Dirty got the introductions out of the way, then sat back and listened as big money spoke.

"Did you like that brick?" Keebler asked.

"I was hoping to get ahold of a couple more for the right price," Twin replied. "With it being the same dope of course," he continued with a slight chuckle. He didn't know it, but he'd just set off alarms in Keebler's head.

"I ain't never seen this Cutlass before. What part of town you from?" Keebler asked as he watched the man and tried to get a read on him.

"North Memphis bound," Ya-Yo spoke up as he lit the blunt he'd been rolling. "I'm usually always on the block, but my connect been out of pocket recently. This is the first time in a while that I've been off the block," Twin answered honestly.

They continued to converse for a few minutes before Keebler remembered that he had Zya waiting for him. "I got whatever you need. Take my number and hit me up when you ready to get straight," he said, then gave Twin his number. The dopeboy promised to get up with him in the near future, and then both vehicles went separate ways.

***

Zya was just about to call Keebler to see what was taking him so long when the familiar sound of bass shook the establishment. Keebler parked at the same pump and turned down the music.

"What you 'bout to get into?" he asked.

"Shit, go to the house to see what Midnight been having a attitude about," Dirty said sadly.

"Remember, young nigga: a happy wife is a happy home," Keebler said before laughing at the expression on his young hitman's face.

"I know," Dirty admitted, then hopped out the car.

Keebler got out the car and found Zya watching him with a huge smile on her face. He waited up until Dirty was safely in the car and pulling off in the afternoon traffic before going in the gas station.

9

It took Flea no time to find the vehicle he was looking for. There was a silver Crown Vic with a white half top that called for his attention, and Flea was already envisioning how it would look with the lift kit. After a quick test drive, both the car salesman and Flea were happy with the outcome. The salesman was happy because he'd just sold a car for cash money, and Flea was now headed back to South Memphis in his new ride. Before he got back to the hood, his homeboy Big Dee was hitting him up.

"What up, Dee?" Flea answered on the second ring.

"Where you at? It ain't like you to miss no money," Big Dee asked. The track had been rolling, and he'd been on the hustle ever since Keebler and Krash fronted him two bricks.

"I just bought a car, nigga. I'm on my way to pick up the rims I got so I can bolt up," Flea bragged. "I know you getting money now, but I want you to ride with me," he continued.

When Flea pulled up on the block, it was business as usual from what he could see. Money was being made, but all eyes were on the unfamiliar silver car stopped in the middle of the street. Flea didn't want to get shot at by any of the paranoid hustlers, so he calmly pulled up at his traphouse and jumped out with the factory sound system blasting.

Immediately, hustlers walked over to check out the ride, but there were other things on Flea's mind. He found a junkie and had him load the 26-inch rims in the backseat while looking for his best friend.

Moments later, Big Dee came strutting up the street with a huge smile on his face.

"What got you so happy?" Flea asked.

"I just sold my first kilo for $23,000," Big Dee said before pulling out the money to show he was serious.

"Put that up before you get us both laid out," Flea demanded. He motioned for them to get in the car, already knowing everybody outside saw his friend with all that money. The factory radio had a CD player, which was blasting Flea's mixtape. Knowing they were being watched, Flea slowly backed out the driveway and sped off, burning rubber.

The first stop they made was at Jay's Audio Sales to get a custom sound system put in the car and some limo tint around the windows.

Flea knew one of the owners, so they made a deal to hook the hustler up in exchange for some weed.

While the owner had one of his employees hook Flea up, they went to the office to smoke a Hydro blunt. Big Dee couldn't believe the royal treatment his friend was getting. Since he'd really just started selling dope when he got fronted, he was still learning the game. Now that he had money in his pocket, he was determined not to fall back off on his hustle game.

Two hours and two blunts later, Flea was back in traffic and headed to a small shop owned by a dude he went to school with. The system sounded so good to the hustlers that they had to fight falling asleep to the sound of the deep bass pounding in the trunk.

"I can't wait 'til I can afford a car," Big Dee yelled over the music. That comment made Flea mute the music and turn serious.

"I know you infatuated with the lifestyle, and it's tempting to spend the money in your pocket, but you need to pay Keebler and Krash whatever you owe them," he stated firmly.

The look Big Dee gave him said more than words could have. He had been thinking of not paying the men who fronted him the two kilos. He felt that a pistol would solve any problems that stemmed from his betrayal, and Flea knew what was on his mind.

"You don't want the trouble that'll come behind what you thinking about doing," Flea explained.

Just as they pulled up at the mechanic shop, Flea realized what he had to do in order to keep his friend from getting hurt in the future. While his car went on the rack, he texted his partner his whereabouts.

Big Dee sat next to him the entire time higher than cloud nine and clueless about what was going on around him. He was busy watching the mechanic put a lift kit on the Crown Victoria while imagining how his game with the females would change if he had a car like his best friend.

Flea got the text he was looking for just as the mechanic was finishing up with the car. Smiling, he glanced over and realized he had to wake up Big Dee, who'd dozed off.

"Let's ride out," Flea said as he led the way to where his car was now parked as the mechanic wiped it down with a dry cloth.

For a moment, both hustlers slowly walked around the car admiring how good it looked sitting up on the 26-inch wheels.

"You can give them old niggas a run for their money," Big Dee said, speaking on Keebler and Krash.

"Let's roll out," Flea told his best friend as he climbed in the driver's seat. It was time that Big Dee learned a valuable lesson of the hustle game, something he needed to know if he planned on prospering in the future. He knew Big Dee would be mad at him for a while, but it was something he'd deal with in order to keep his best friend safe.

"Where we going?" Big Dee asked upon seeing they weren't headed toward South Memphis.

"Out east," Flea said then turned up the music. He was now in full flexing mode, so he passed some weed to Big Dee for him to roll up.

***

At the gas station, Keebler listened to Zya as she cried about already missing her favorite cousin Godzilla. She even told him how she was talking to Calvin, and while he was explaining what he'd seen at the scene, gunshots were heard in the background before the phone went dead.

"Did he call back?" Keebler asked with fake sincerity. He knew who the shots she'd heard had come from. He just wanted to make sure Dirty finished the job.

"I tried calling him back a few times, but it just keep going to the voicemail," Zya replied. Although she didn't say it, she knew he was dead too, and all the murders were tied together somehow.

They spoke a little while longer about how she felt about the death of Godzilla with Keebler texting a few times here and there before changing the subject.

"So, what do you got planned for us today?" Zya asked with that same seductive look in her eyes that first got Keebler's attention.

He was about to say something slick until he spotted a certain vehicle flexing up Winchester, headed directly at him.

"I know my young nigga didn't," Keebler mumbled as his legs led him from behind the counter and toward the door.

Seeing another Crown Victoria sitting on 26-inch wheels wasn't uncommon in the city, but Keebler knew it had to be Flea. When he first pulled up at the car lot, the half top caught his eyes immediately. Now, only hours after he'd last seen the young hustler, seeing the car customized with a slamming sound system made him nod his head in approval as he watched the car buck traffic to get on the lot.

"Who is that?" Zya asked while looking at how clean the car was.

"That's one of my young niggas," Keebler replied, then walked outside just as the car parked in front of his.

Inside the car, Big Dee's high had just been blown when he spotted the blue Crown Vic parked at the gas pump. He looked over at Flea with pleading eyes like it would kill him to keep it real.

"Pay my nigga what you owe him," Flea said in a brotherly tone. "You never bite the hand that feed you, bruh, no matter how tempting it is. This is the type of nigga you want on your team," he continued as Keebler stood outside the car patiently.

Big Dee thought about it for a moment, then decided his best friend was right. He still had a little less than a brick left, so everything he made now was all profit. "That's why you my nigga," Big Dee said before giving Flea dap. Then the men stepped out the car looking and smelling like money.

"Let me find out you trying to hang with the big dogs," Keebler said, smiling as he walked around the car to get a better look. He silently admired the top but tried not to make it look so obvious.

"I think I surpassed trying," Flea said as he walked over to give the man dap.

"Did you ride all the way to the eastside to flex on a old man, or is this business?" Keebler asked when he noticed Big Dee.

"I got business, but I think it's a little bit of both with dude," Big Dee said with a smile. "I got that bread for you," he continued.

"You got rid of both of those thangs already?" Keebler asked, surprised.

"I still got a little bit to work with, but a wise man once told me to never bite the hand that feed you," Big Dee said, quoting what had just been told to him.

"Y'all come inside so we don't have people all in our business," Keebler said, then led the way inside the gas station.

***

After a good nap, Krash was energized and ready to hit the streets. He was surprised his best friend hadn't called or been by the house, so after making a thick cup of Folgers coffee, he called his right hand.

"I thought you'd fell off the face of the earth," the voice he was looking for answered as a greeting.

"I had to deal with Trina, and we both fell asleep," Krash said between sips of coffee.

"As usual, while sis got you on lockdown, I'm out here keeping us afloat," Keebler said as a way of letting the man know there was money in the works without saying too much on the phone.

"I'm about to get into traffic. Where you at?" Krash asked, now energized.

As Keebler explained what his day had been like since they parted ways, Krash got ready to hit the streets.

"I'll be your way in a minute," Krash said, dressed for the town. He ended the call, then kissed his girl softly on the forehead, making sure to lock the door and set the alarm on the house on his way out.

***

Zya tried not to be nosey as the men handled business like they owned the place, but it was hard when so much money was changing hands. Big Dee counted out twenty grand and gave it to Keebler, who recounted it. He did this to teach the young hustler to always double-check his money when doing business, and he explained why.

"Trust nobody when it comes to money. Business is always business, no matter how good of a personal relationship you may have with that person," Keebler said. He was schooling the young hustler on the ethics of a true hustler because when Flea texted him, he told him his best friend was thinking about keeping the money. Because Flea had spoken so highly of the man, he was willing to give him some game.

If it had been anyone else that even thought about taking something from him after he had taken a chance on them, Keebler would've killed him just for the thought. Flea knew this much and decided to take matters into his own hands when he figured out what his best friend was thinking about. Now, everybody was on the same page in his eyes, but Keebler had a surprise up his sleeve.

"You want some more work?" he asked.

Big Dee was very shocked at the question, but he kept his cool. He thought about if he should try his luck again or just be content with whatever he made from the rest of the dope he had left.

"I know about what you thought about doing, young nigga," Keebler said, reading his mind. "I've killed niggas for less, so if that's the road you wanna take, so be it. I'm offering you a permanent connection through me, and I promise if anybody disrespect your hustle, then my niggas will handle it. On the same token, if you steal one dollar from me, not even Flea will be able to save you next time," he continued.

"I can't lie. When I saw my nigga bolting up, the thought of putting you on hold so I can get a whip did cross my mind," Big Dee said honestly. "I'm actually glad my nigga kept me on the right path because I do see that keeping it real goes both ways. Send another brick my way and until I can build up my clientele. We'll just work brick to brick," he continued, careful not to put too much on his plate.

"Deal," Keebler said and put his arm around the young hustler. The way he'd just kept it real made Keebler promise himself that he would take the young nigga up under his wing in the future. "I'll have that brought to you first thing in the morning," Keebler promised.

Flea was ready to hit the streets, so he told Keebler to get at them later on, and then they left.

Not long after Flea left the gas station, Krash pulled up with his system on blast.

"Y'all can start a car club with them cars as clean as they are," Zya said.

"We might just do that," Keebler replied just as his best friend walked in.

"We might just do what?" Krash asked hesitantly as he showed Keebler some love.

"Baby think we should start up a car club. You'll see why later," Keebler said, then nodded for them to step outside.

"You know I'm about to get off," Zya blurted out. She didn't want the men to leave.

"We'll just be outside talking," Keebler promised, then led the way outside.

"What's the business?" Krash asked once they were alone.

***

Dirty made it home safely and found Midnight listening to rap music on the computer.

"Hey babe," she said with a smile while dancing in her chair.

Dirty found himself bobbing his head to the music. "Who is that?" he asked as he walked up to look at the screen. Midnight was on Facebook listening to music that Flea had on his page.

"When I saw him earlier, I knew his face from somewhere," she explained.

Dirty just stared at the screen while listening to how good the music sounded. "I'm surprised he didn't say nothing when we were in the south," Dirty said. "Can you download that?" he asked.

"Yes, but this is his last mixtape. He should have something else out by now," Midnight replied.

"Still, get that, and we'll ride by the south side later. Just remind me to ask about the CD," Dirty said. "Oh! That's fifty grand. Put that up for me," he continued as he pulled out the money he'd made from the lick at the traphouse.

While Midnight did what she was asked to do, Dirty went to take a quick shower. He had plans of getting back in the streets, and he wanted to look up to par when he did.

***

By the time Keebler finished telling Krash what his day had been about, he found his best friend momentarily speechless.

"So, you got 25 bricks and fifty grand in the trunk right now?" Krash asked.

"Yeah. Plus the twenty grand from the nigga we fronted the two bricks to," Keebler said as he pulled out the bankroll. He slowly counted out ten thousand to give his best friend before repocketing the rest.

"You know you don't need to be riding around with all that shit," Krash cautiously stated.

Right then, Zya walked outside with her purse on her shoulder ready to go.

"We about to go drop that off now and pick sis up in the process," Keebler said before hitting the remote starter on his key ring.

"I guess I'm following you then," Krash said as he hit his remote starter as well. They hopped in the cars and left.

***

Flea took the scenic route back to the hood just so he could flex.

"You hitting the block tonight or are you hanging out with me at the studio?" Flea muted the music and asked.

For a moment, Big Dee was in deep thought. He wanted to get about his money, but he knew Flea always splurged when he made music. That was why the music always sounded so good.

"Kick it with me tonight. I got you," Flea said, making the decision even harder.

"Fuck it! I'm chilling with you," Big Dee decided with a smile.

"I'll just make a quick stop in the hood to get us some weed to blow on. Then we off the map for the night," Flea said, then turned the system back up.

10

The original plan was for Flea to pull up in the hood and grab some weed for them to blow on while they were at the studio, then dip off undetected. As soon as he pulled up on the scene, he knew pulling in and out wasn't happening. All the hustlers who were out making money eased over to admire how clean the car was. Before Flea stepped out the Crown Vic, the vehicle was surrounded by people admiring the huge rims on the car while others expressed how good the system sounded. Since Big Dee was still chilling in the car, Flea slipped away from the crowd to go to his stash.

To his surprise, there were even more people out when he stepped back outside. While Flea answered any questions thrown at him about his car, he got Big Dee to twist up a couple of blunts for them to blow on as they headed to the studio.

Thirty minutes later, they were still parked in the hood with the system blasting his latest traphouse mixtape when Flea spotted a familiar vehicle come speeding up the street. As soon as the vehicle was spotted by the hustlers, they all cleared out like the police were doing a sweep.

Standing there with a smile on his face, Flea patiently waited for his new friend to step up to his car.

"I see you didn't waste no time putting them shoes to some good use," Dirty stepped up and said with a smile as he gave Flea dap. "And I like your choice of ride. It's about time somebody showed them old heads that us young niggas can show out too," he continued as he walked around the car.

Hearing the bass pounding from the trunk reminded Dirty that he needed to ask about his music, but Flea was currently busy on the phone, so he waited. He could hear him saying something about going to the studio, and he wanted to go as well. As soon as Flea ended the call, Dirty was about to ask if he could hang out with him at the studio, but Flea beat him to the question.

"You got anything planned for tonight?" Flea asked.

"Me and the missus were going to get about our hustle, but I'd love to kick it with my new homeboy," Dirty said, sounding like a teenager.

"Good! I just got off the phone with Keebler. Him and big bruh bringing their girls to the studio, and I want you to hang out with me," Flea explained.

"I guess I'm following you then," Dirty said. "You wouldn't happen to have one of your mixtapes on you, would you? Lil mama infatuated with your music and told me to ask if you'd sell us a CD," he continued.

Just hearing that the goddess Flea had secretly thought about since last seeing her liked his music was motivation for the young hustler. "I keep a couple with me at all times," Flea said as he led the way to the car. "I don't feel right putting a charge to my guy, so this one is on me," he continued as he gave Dirty his latest mixtape. Without saying another word, the two groups sped off into the night.

***

While Keebler led the way to Coro Lake, he decided to call Flea and pre-order a package to smoke on. It was then that they made other plans to meet up and kick it at the studio where Flea made his music. Since Flea promised to supply the group with all the weed they wanted to smoke, Keebler decided to bring something for them to drink on. After getting the address to the studio, Keebler ended the call and turned his attention to Zya, who was relaxing in the passenger seat.

"So, what do you think would be the best drink for you to sip on at the studio?" he asked. He quickly explained why they were hanging out at a studio, pointing out that the music they were currently listening to was the person they were going to meet up with.

"How many females will be there?" Zya asked.

"You and Trina as far as I know," Keebler said.

The fact that Zya would have a female friend to keep her company was all she needed to hear. "Well, I'm game to drink whatever Trina wanna drink," Zya replied. The look she gave Keebler showed how much she was still hurting from losing her cousin, but she was trying not to think about it so much.

When they pulled up to the house, Keebler was shocked to find Trina in a good mood. As he pulled the duffelbag from the trunk, he found Zya already at the door in deep conversation with both Krash and Trina. Already sensing what the topic of conversation, Keebler felt good seeing his future girlfriend fit in with the only family he had.

"So, I hear you're treating us girls to some drinks," Trina said playfully as Keebler strutted up the steps.

"You know how I do, sis," he replied calmly. He led the way into the house like it was his own and went to the back office, already knowing that only Krash was following.

Once the men were alone, Krash took control of the situation. "What's this I hear about us hanging out at some studio?" he asked as he took the duffelbag and emptied the contents on the desk.

***

Nothing was said in the Crown Vic until they were safely in traffic with two blunts in the air. Then, Big Dee spoke his mind.

"Flea, why are you fucking with dude and you know he ain't straight?" he asked.

"Who?" Flea asked with surprise like he didn't know who his best friend was talking about.

"Dirty, nigga!" Big Dee yelled as he took a quick look in his mirror to see if the Beamer was still following them.

"Dirty is straight, my nigga," Flea calmly replied with a smile. He glanced over at his friend and saw real terror in his eyes. "Do you remember that promise Keebler made earlier?" he asked. Because Big Dee was so high, Flea paused to let the man replay the earlier events in his head. "He's one of the niggas he was talking about," Flea said when Big Dee smiled.

"So, I don't have to worry about whether Dirty will rob me?" Big Dee asked. The question made Flea laugh, and he saw how he hurt his best friend's feelings, so he explained.

"First of all, don't take what I'm about to say the wrong way, but you ain't the type of person Dirty is known for getting at," Flea said. "Secondly, you plugged in with the big brothers, so taking from you is like taking from them," he explained. Big Dee thought about what Flea told him and began to relax in the comfort of knowing he was part of something for once in his life.

***

Because Krash and Keebler had the habit of never trusting anyone outside of their circle, they always recounted the money they made, and they were doing it again. Once they were both satisfied that the fifty grand and 25 kilos were accounted for, Krash put everything in the floor safe in the office.

"Let's go see if the girls are ready to ride out," Krash suggested.

"That sounds good because I need to stop at a liquor store before they close for the night," Keebler replied. "By the way, we riding with you tonight so I can concentrate on my baby," he continued as they went to find the girls.

Krash just laughed as a reply because he knew the real truth. Keebler liked to drink just as much as he enjoyed getting high. With a designated driver secured, there was no limit to how much he could enjoy himself.

The girls were in the living room smoking on a blunt and chit-chatting like they owned the world. "Where y'all get some weed from?" Keebler asked as he took the blunt out of Trina's hand.

"I know how to hold weed, unlike you," Trina said as she took the blunt back. "This blunt is for us. If you wanna smoke, you'll have to roll your own," she continued.

"My bad, sis. Damn!" Keebler said in his brotherly tone.

Zya laughed at the pitiful look on her man's face. As down as she had been feeling about Godzilla being killed, it kind of surprised her how the people she'd just met days before made her feel like family.

"Y'all ready to roll out?" Krash spoke up with a smile. He already knew that when Keebler and Trina were together, anything was possible. As everyone got up to leave, he only hoped that whoever would be at the studio was prepared for the show that was about to go down once his two most favorite people got intoxicated.

***

The place Flea considered a studio was one of his homeboys' houses. One of the bedrooms had been transformed into the place where unknown rappers attempted to make a name for themselves. After the owner of the studio first heard Flea spit bars on the mic, he immediately saw the potential and made the young hustler a deal that even Flea knew not to refuse. That was the beginning of a new friendship, and both men had held up their ends of the deal. Now, Flea was pulling up at the house with the music on blast, only to realize there was already a session in progress as he viewed the various vehicles parked around the house.

"Your boy know we coming?" Big Dee asked as he parked at the curb.

"I got a open invitation, homie. I don't never have to make an appointment," Flea replied. "Come on. Let's get out so you can meet Dirty," he continued as he hopped out the car.

The first thing he noticed was the beauty Midnight possessed as they all met up at the end of the driveway. Flea had to look away to keep from staring and risking his life for the love he was feeling for this stranger whom he knew he just had to get to know.

"Big Dee, this is my dude Dirty," Flea made the introductions, then led the way to the house without waiting for the men to give each other dap.

The sound of music could be heard on the other side of the front door, and the tempo had them moving their heads to the beat. Flea knocked on the door, then waited for his friend to let them in.

A bald black man opened the door seconds after hearing the knock.

"What's up, Kojak?" Flea greeted the man with his hand out.

"As the O'Jays say it: *money, money, money, money*," Kojak sang as he shook his hand. Flea quickly introduced everyone in his group.

"I have a few more people who should be pulling up shortly," Flea said.

"It's all good, man. Come on in and get comfortable. I should be finished with the session I'm in now in about an hour," Kojak said as he led the way inside the house.

Dirty quickly glanced around the studio at the other occupants, trying to see if he had beef with anyone. The huge bulge under his shirt plus the mean mug on his face let everybody know how he got down. Almost immediately, the whispering and head nodding began once people started to notice who he was, but he just shook it off. If they knew who he was, it was understood how he got down. His only concern was how the owner of the house would feel about him being there once word got back to him about how Dirty got down in the streets.

Kojak immediately went back to working with the young rappers already in the booth, so Flea sat back and got comfortable.

"Roll up," he said suddenly before pulling out a huge Ziploc bag of what he called Mad Dog Kush. "This is a new shipment I just got ahold of. We the first people to sample this shit, so let me know what you think," Flea said. He was speaking to Dirty and Big Dee, but his eyes were on Midnight, who couldn't stop blushing like a little girl.

"This shit smells good," Dirty said while eyeing the weed through the bag. It was a dark green color with deep red veins running through it, and it had a smell that was very intoxicating.

"I've been getting complaints from a few niggas who can't afford my Hydro prices, so I copped some of this to sell at regular prices," Flea explained.

"Well, if it smokes like it smells, I want a pound of this shit in the morning," Dirty said as he pulled out a couple of buds to roll before passing the sack to Big Dee. He noticed there were no sticks or seeds in the weed and knew it was a good grade.

***

The studio was located deep in the east side, and Keebler knew that if they waited until they got to the area, the liquor stores would be closed for the night.

"Stop so I can get something to drink," he said suddenly.

"I'm already on top of that," Krash replied just as he pulled up at a liquor store on Winchester.

"What are you ladies drinking, sis?" Keebler asked once they were parked.

"Get some Thug Passion Alizé," Trina said after she made sure it was cool with Zya.

Keebler quickly checked his pistol to make sure he had a round in the chamber, then hopped out the car like he didn't have a care in the world.

"Does he always have a gun on him?" Zya asked suddenly.

"Yep," Trina and Krash said at the same time, then laughed.

***

It didn't take long for people to start asking about the weed once the aroma started circulating around the studio.

"That's you who got it smelling like paradise in here?" Kojak asked with a smile.

"You know I keep something circulating," Flea replied loud enough for everyone in the house to hear. Getting money was all he knew, and even when he was having fun, he was still working.

"How about you share some of that weed if you like to keep something circulating," a fat man who'd been eyeing the group since they got to the house stated firmly. He'd heard what the people were whispering, but since he'd never heard of Dirty himself, he took the rumors to be just that.

"I don't think you want none of this weed right here," Big Dee spoke up as he stood up. Although he wasn't as big as the man trying to scare Flea, he did have some size on him, and there was no doubt about how in shape Big Dee was.

"Why is that, young nigga?" the fat man asked with a smile. He found it funny that the one person nobody spoke about had the nerve to stand up to him.

"Because that weed there got blood on it," Dirty said before stepping up next to Big Dee.

The fat man weighed his options. He was thinking about trying the men, but a voice in the back of his mind pleaded for him to fall back, so he did.

Since Flea was more hustler than gangster, he pulled out some buds and passed them around to everyone in the studio. Kojak smiled at his friend, then turned to everyone in the house.

"Because my nigga fucking with y'all, don't take that as him being weak. His homeboys could instantly make you famous, but my guy is more of a peace maker," Kojak spoke firmly.

Flea was thanked for showing love, but the fat man took it as though he'd scared the hustler. Dirty had it made up in his mind already that the man had to be dealt with, and he made a vow to himself to handle the issue as soon as he left the studio. The sound of the doorbell made Flea smile because he already knew who was at the door.

Since Kojak was told to expect more visitors, as soon as he heard the doorbell, he went to answer it. He'd noticed the look Dirty had given the fat man. Now he just hoped nobody tore his house up while he was at the door.

The first things Kojak noticed were the two sexy women standing next to men who looked like hustlers. He was already having enough trouble keeping the people in his house from killing each other. The last thing he needed was to have his own personal enemies lurking around.

"What's good?" Kojak asked in his cool tone.

"My dude Flea invited us to a session," Keebler spoke up. Kojak explained that they were waiting for them to show up.

"Just follow the smell of the Kush," he said as he stepped aside to let them in. Since they weren't used to the environment, Krash led the way with the girls in the middle and Keebler taking up the rear.

"It's smelling good as a muthafucka in here," Krash said as he noticed some familiar faces. Flea immediately went over and gave the men dap.

"You know I keep some good shit," Flea boasted.

At first, he was uncomfortable being outnumbered at the studio with all the tension in the air. Now, with the big dogs around, Flea felt a lot better about the odds if something did pop off. Dirty and Midnight spoke to everyone except Zya because they didn't know her. Keebler quickly introduced her as his girlfriend, making her blush, but Keebler didn't notice because of the look Dirty had in his eyes. That was his little brother, and he knew when he wanted to put in some work. He had to get to the bottom of things just in case it had something to do with Flea or Big Dee.

"Damn! We need some more cigars before I jump in this booth," Flea said upon realizing they had the last two cigars in rotation.

"I got a couple of Optimos," Trina spoke up, ready to smoke.

"Y'all roll on up. Me and Keebler will ride off to the store right quick," Dirty suggested suddenly. He'd noticed that the group that was at the studio when they got there was preparing to leave, and that included the fat man. Keebler seemed to be the only person who caught on to the urgency in the young hitman's voice, so he agreed to ride with him. Krash was a vet in the game, and he'd survived so long was because he'd been able to sense when danger was lurking.

"I'll walk you to the door," Krash said in a deep drawl while already following the men to the door. Nobody spoke until they were at the Beamer.

"What's going on?" Krash asked suddenly.

"That fat boy in there stepped to Flea like he wanted to take something," Dirty explained. "Me and Big Dee had to step up, and it almost got physical," he continued. Both Keebler and Krash instantly got mad at the thought of some nigga disrespecting someone they called family.

"So, what's the deal?" Krash asked while already forming an idea of what was about to happen.

"Me and big bruh gone follow these fools, and the first opportunity we get, that fat boy gotta pay for his disrespect," Dirty admitted.

"Say no more. Just make sure y'all handle the business and get out of there," Krash stated firmly. "And Keebler, don't be on no extra shit. You already know how you do," he continued with a laugh.

"Just make sure Midnight is safe," Dirty said as he hopped behind the wheel of the car.

"I'll guard her with my own life," Krash promised, then stepped back so the men could pull off. It was a good thing they'd already left because as Krash went back in the house, the fat man and his crew were walking out. It actually took everything Krash had in him not to step to the man for disrespecting Flea, but because he already knew what the future held for the man, he went on about his business.

11

As the fat man and his crew headed to their car, he was tempted to take a closer look at the customized Crown Vics parked at the curb.

"I like the silver one with the half top," one of the men said.

"They both are clean, but that red one got some gold flakes twinkling off the paint job," the fat man replied. He was beginning to not only wonder who the group in the studio was, but if he should test them to see what he could get. He decided to let the men be, but if they happened to cross paths again, he would step to them. Without a care in the world, they hopped in their vehicle and sped off, unaware that there was someone on their tail.

Parked at the end of the block was the BMW, already in gear. Dirty wanted to be as inconspicuous as possible while handling this business, but there was no way he was letting the man get away with his bold disrespect.

"So, what we doing? We hitting all of them or just the fat boy?" Keebler asked.

"I was always taught that birds of a feather stick together. In my eyes, that makes them guilty by association," Dirty replied confidently.

"Say no more," Keebler calmly said just as the targets pulled away from the house.

Dirty waited a few seconds, then pulled off behind them. They made sure not to follow too close to avoid causing suspicion, and once they were in the late-night traffic, it became easier to follow. When the vehicle they were following pulled up at a Checkers drive-thru, Dirty quickly turned into some rundown apartments.

"What you doing?" Keebler asked.

"Just be cool and get ready to hop out," Dirty said while speeding through the deserted apartments.

After finding a parking space by a tree that hid the black Beamer in case someone happened to ride by, the men hopped out with Glocks in hand. Since Dirty knew where to go, he led the way through several breezeways that eventually came out right behind the Checkers. To their surprise, the car was just pulling up to the speaker to order. Slowly and quietly, Dirty and Keebler when through a hole in the fence. Without warning, they ran up on both sides of the car to the open windows.

Boc! Boc! Boc! Boc! Boc! Boc! Boc! Boc!

The shots seemed to go on forever as multiple shots hit everyone in the vehicle. Without warning, Keebler turned to the vehicle that was already at the drive-thru window picking up food.

Boc! Boc! Boc! Boc!

When the back window shattered, the vehicle sped off into the night traffic, trying to escape the barrage of bullets.

"Let's go!" Dirty yelled over his shoulder as he ran off behind the restaurant. Keebler caught up to him just as they reached the hole in the fence and disappeared into the night.

Once they were back in the car, Dirty sped off but left the headlights off as he headed back out the apartments. It wasn't until they were back in traffic that Dirty turned the lights on.

"Why did you shoot at the other car?" he asked suddenly.

"Just a little insurance to make sure they mind their own business in case they were trying to get a look at us," Keebler explained. "I would have killed them if I wanted to," he continued. Dirty glanced at him and laughed.

"Let's get these cigars and get back to the studio so we can have our alibis," Keebler said as he pushed his seat back to get comfortable.

***

Back at the house, Flea was showing off, playing some unheard music that he'd made. The girls were sipping on Alizé and enjoying themselves while the men played with the equipment.

"I want a copy of this shit, and I won't take no for an answer," Krash said.

"This shit we hearing now is still being edited, but you know I got y'all once we get it right," Flea replied.

"Unless you plan on laying something down tonight, we can finish the editing," Kojak spoke up from where he sat in front of the computer.

"When have I not wanted to lay something down?" Flea asked cockily. "I got something together for that last track you made," he continued.

"The booth is open now if you ready," Kojak said while already uploading the instrumental to be recorded. Instead of replying, Flea headed into the booth and put on the headphones.

Seconds later, the track started playing, so he went to work.

"It's a dirty game; dirty world, but still, I'm in it,/

Hanging on da block; wit my chrome, committing sins,/

In this fast lane; who's to say I'm gone succeed,/

When it's a fifty chance; I might die off in them streets."

By the time Flea had finished dropping the track, the girls were into the music, but Midnight couldn't seem to take her eyes away from the recording booth. Zya was the first to notice how much Midnight was into Flea, so she got Trina's attention.

"Either that Alizé and good weed we smoking got Midnight in a daze, or she has a thing for that boy in the booth," she whispered to Trina. They both started watching Midnight with smiles on their faces until they were busted.

"Why you hoes watching me and shit?" Midnight asked while blushing at the fact that she'd been caught watching Flea.

"Shit, I don't blame you, girl," Trina said suddenly. "It's something about that skinny-ass boy that can get you hooked without you knowing it. Just don't let Dirty's bad ass catch on to them feelings," she continued in a sisterly tone.

"I have no intention of leaving my man, but I have to get some of him," Midnight admitted.

"Just be careful, girl. The heart can sometimes have a mind of its own," Zya gave her two cents.

Midnight was about to ask Zya what she meant by her comment when Dirty and Keebler entered the studio in the middle of a conversation of their own.

Keebler had a brown paper bag in his hand as he sat down next to Zya.

"Did you miss me?" he asked with a smile.

"You know I did," Zya said seductively as she gave him a passionate kiss.

"What's in the bag, bruh?" Trina asked.

Keebler pulled out a two-liter Coke and four boxes of cigars. "Where that weed at?" Keebler asked as he began busting open a cigar. He needed a blunt to smoke on while he sipped on Hennessy and Coke to ease his nerves. He noticed Krash watching him and nodded twice to let him know that the business had been handled. For the rest of the night, they all stayed at the studio watching Flea make his music.

*   *   *

The smell of bacon woke Keebler up. It took a minute for him to figure out where he was and how he'd gotten there.

"I gotta stop drinking," he told himself as he climbed out of bed, only to realize he was still fully dressed. The sudden smell of blunts in the air filled his nostrils as soon as he opened the bedroom door, so he followed the sounds of female laughter that led him to the kitchen.

"Look who finally woke up," Trina said cheerfully.

"Morning, sweetie," Zya said as she walked over to her man and kissed him on the cheek. Before he could ask, she passed the already lit blunt to him, then led him to a seat at the breakfast table. As Keebler sat down, he noticed his best friend sitting at the table with a huge smile on his face.

"What you smiling at?" Keebler asked. Zya placed a plate full of food in front of him, then left the men in the kitchen.

"Do you remember anything about last night?" Krash asked once they were alone.

"I remember putting in that work with lil bruh," Keebler replied.

"What about afterward?" Krash asked with a smile.

As Keebler thought about the night before, he was sure it couldn't have been too bad because his best friend had a big smile on his face.

"I can't lie. Shit got fuzzy once I started drinking," Keebler admitted.

"All I can say is I hope I'm the best man at the wedding," Krash said slowly so his best friend would catch on to what he was saying. Keebler was in the middle of hitting the blunt when he heard the comment and choked on the weed.

"What the fuck you say?" he asked between coughs.

As Krash replayed the events from the night before, Keebler listened intently. He now understood why he had a smile on his face.

"Well, they say a drunk man can tell no lie," Keebler replied. "Maybe I need to settle down and focus on this money," he continued.

"Speaking of money. Are we pushing on your target today or what?" Krash asked. He knew they would have to handle the business soon enough, so he figured they should get it out of the way. "It's the perfect time to move since all the attention is either out north or on the east side right now," Krash explained.

"How about we put it off until tomorrow?" Keebler suggested. "That'll give me time to get the rides and have everything in position. You know I hate to go at anything blind," he continued.

Krash laughed so hard, he spit food out of his mouth, but since he didn't feel like debating, he left the subject alone. "So, what're we doing today?" he asked.

***

On the other side of town, Dirty was already up and dressed for the day.

"Where you going?" Midnight asked after rolling over to find her man out of bed.

"I need to go holler at Twin," Dirty said.

Midnight was still sleepy, so she went back to sleep while her man continued to get ready for the day. It had been a long time since the young hitman ran around in the streets during the day, so he was anxious to see how people would react when seeing him, although he already knew it would be like other times when hustlers avoided him. Deciding to ride with a new pistol, Dirty chose a nickel-plated P-30 Glock. He took five grand for spending money, then locked up the house as he headed to the car.

As soon as he was in traffic, he made a phone call.

"What up?" Flea answered on the third ring. He was quite surprised to see Dirty calling him so early.

"I was just getting into traffic, and I wanted to know if I could come cop that weed we spoke about last night," Dirty said.

"I think I need to find me a Denny's sign to hang over the crib," Flea replied.

"What for?" Dirty asked, not catching the joke.

"Because, nigga! The trap stays open 24/7," the hustler said, making both of them laugh.

"Well, I gotta make a quick stop in North Memphis. Then I'm on my way to you," Dirty said. The two men continued talking for several more minutes before hanging up.

Dirty had been so deep in the conversation that when he finally ended the call, he was already on the north side of town. After turning down Bickford Avenue, he spotted his cousin's Cutlass parked in a driveway up the street from the neighborhood traphouse. Thinking

Twin just parked there to keep the police from harassing him about how clean the car was, Dirty almost went on to the traphouse, but something made him pull over. As he looked around before he hopped out the Beamer, he noticed everything looked a little too calm, so he cocked his P-30 to make sure a round was in the chamber. Just as he stepped out the car, Twin stepped out of the house with a female under his arm.

"Who is that?" Dirty heard the female ask.

"That's my lil cousin," Twin said with a smile just as they met up at the Cutlass. "What got you out this way so damn early in the daytime?" Twin asked while giving his cousin dap.

"I can't come holler at my family?" Dirty asked with a smile.

"I guess so," Twin replied hesitantly. "If you wanna kick it, you gotta be willing to ride around with me," he continued as he hit the alarm on the Cutlass.

"Where you expect me to leave my whip?" Dirty asked. "You know how niggas get whenever they think I'm in the hood," he continued, letting his cousin know about the rumors floating around the city.

Twin thought about it before turning his attention to the young lady who was still standing out. "Can you keep an eye on my cousin's car?" he asked.

"Bring me something to smoke," the female replied.

"I'll do you better than that," Dirty spoke up. He pulled out his bankroll and peeled off a one-hundred-dollar bill. "Get you something to smoke with this, and I'll still bring back a sack for you," he said as he gave the female the money. She quickly agreed, then watched as the men switched parking spots. Once Dirty knew his car was locked up with the alarm on, he hopped in the Cutlass with Twin, and they sped off.

Because Krash and Keebler were so close, Keebler always kept clothes at the spot in case he needed to change. Now dressed for success, the men were back in traffic, only this time, they were in the blue Crown Vic.

"Did you bring that brick with you?" Keebler muted the system and asked.

"Yeah, I got it," Krash replied before pulling a brown paper bag from under the seat.

"What about the personal?" Keebler asked. It had been a minute since either man had snorted cocaine, and they were missing that high.

"I brought a half a zip. That'll definitely last us throughout the day," Krash replied just as he pulled out two crispy one-hundred-dollar bills.

While he filled the bills with powder, Keebler changed the CD and popped in the disc Flea had downloaded for them at the studio. When they pulled up at a red light, Keebler got his powder and took several snorts to get the feeling he was looking for. Once he caught a drain, he turned up the music and let the system blast as they headed to South Memphis.

***

Word had quickly spread about the new weed Flea had on the market, and business was booming on the block. Flea noticed that everybody on the block was getting money, but he was getting the most.

"Give me a good deal on a pound of that new weed you got," Big Dee walked up and said after he'd just sold an ounce of powder cocaine.

"That depends," Flea said with a smile. "Is it for profit or pleasure?" he asked.

"I'm on a mission right now," Big Dee replied. He was now running low on cocaine, and he didn't know when to expect Keebler to bring the next brick. The way he was looking at it, with two kinds of drugs on hand, he'd always be making money. Just as he was about to tell his homeboy what his plan was, Keebler came swerving up on the block with the system on blast.

Another customer pulled up for some weed, so Flea went to make the serve while Keebler parked behind the silver Crown Vic that was parked at the curb in front of the traphouse. Although Krash had seen the car the night before, it looked totally different under the sunlight.

"Is that Flea's whip?" he asked as they hopped out the car. "The young nigga is trying to give us a run for our money," Krash continued as he stepped over to the car.

"That's what my baby was talking about when she said we should start a car club," Keebler explained as he watched Big Dee strut over to them like he was a true baller.

"You just the man we're looking for," Keebler told Big Dee. Without looking so obvious, he passed the brown paper bag to the young hustler.

"We doing the same deal?" Big Dee asked as he cuffed the paper bag.

"As long as I live, you get the discount," Keebler reassured him as he put his arm around the man.

Just as he introduced Big Dee to Krash, the same silver Cutlass that had met up with him the day before pulled up on the block. Since it was a new whip to the hood, the hustlers went on alert, but Keebler already knew who was in the vehicle as it pulled up behind his car.

"Damn! It's live out here in the south," Twin said as soon as he pulled up on the block. He was from the north side of town, and it was very rare that he rode around South Memphis.

"This is where my nigga hustle at," Dirty said proudly. "Let's hop out," he continued once the Cutlass was parked at the curb. The two men hopped out and were immediately greeted by Keebler.

"What you know?" he asked, giving both Dirty and Twin dap while Krash silently stood back watching everything.

"Shit, you just the nigga I'm looking for," Twin replied while smiling. "I need another brick," he continued only loud enough for the group to hear.

"My young nigga may serve you for the fifteen," Keebler said while looking at Big Dee.

It was a quick five-thousand-dollar profit, and Big Dee knew he'd be back straight before the day was out, so he accepted the offer.

"When are you ready to do that?" Big Dee asked, now all business.

"We can do this now. Hop in the whip," Twin said as he led the way back to the Cutlass. Neither man was worried about being robbed because they had Dirty standing guard while they handled the transaction.

When Big Dee pulled the brick of cocaine out of the paper bag, the first thing Twin noticed was the tank logo. He kept his composure, but he wanted to kill Big Dee right on the spot.

"Where you get this from?" Twin asked like he was really interested in the dope. He carefully counted out fifteen grand from his huge bankroll and passed it to Big Dee, who did as Keebler had taught him.

"I got plenty more where that came from," Big Dee boasted once he recounted the money to make sure it was proper.

"Let me get your number so I can hit you up when I need to get straight again," Twin said with a fake smile on his face. He would definitely be back, but it wouldn't be for dope.

Flea stepped up hoping to sneak up on the men but almost regretted it as quick as he thought about doing it. He stepped on a dead leaf, and the crackling sound caused Krash to up his Glock.

"It's just me, big bruh! Don't shoot," Flea said with his hands in the air.

For a moment, Krash just stood there with his Glock aimed at the hustler. When Flea looked him in the eyes, what he saw seared him. It was like everything on the block stopped as they waited to see what was about to happen.

"Fall back, Krash. It's just lil bruh," Keebler spoke up.

It was like hearing Keebler's voice brought Krash back to reality. He shook his head as he lowered the pistol. Once it dawned on him what he'd just done, he couldn't help but smile.

"You know better than to be creeping up on niggas," Krash said as he put his pistol away.

"If he didn't, he know now," Big Dee said as he walked back up on the group.

12

It surprised Dirty when Twin said he was ready to go before he got what they originally drove out there for. He thought it was because they were in South Memphis.

"We straight out here, cuz. Between me and my niggas, a nigga would have to be crazy to jump out on us," Dirty explained.

"That ain't it. I got this work on me, and I just wanna get back to the hood," Twin said with a fake smile. It did make sense so Dirty, so he decided to handle his business.

"You ain't got rid of all that weed, have you?" he asked Flea.

"I got your package in the car," Flea said and led the way to his car. "Just give me five hundred for it," he continued after passing Dirty a Ziploc freezer bag stuffed with the same weed as what he'd smoked the night before. The smell was so intoxicating that Dirty didn't even try to get a cheaper price. He paid five hundred, then headed back to the Cutlass, where his cousin was waiting.

For some reason, Keebler got a bad vibe as they watched the Cutlass speed off the block.

"Yeah," Big Dee said. "He seemed interested in finding out whether I had more work for sale, and I made it sound good," he continued.

Keebler started to think back on the first time he met Twin and how interested he was in the dope. He then turned his attention to Krash.

"Which package did you give the young nigga?" Keebler whispered so only the two of them could hear their conversation.

"It was from the first lick," Krash replied, only confirming what he thought. It was all making more sense to Keebler now, but he was trying to figure out how to tell Dirty that he may have to kill his own cousin.

"Look, I want you to stay away from dude in the Cutlass," Keebler told Big Dee without giving him a valid reason.

"What's going on?" Flea asked as he walked up on the end of the conversation.

"Nothing really. Just a little precaution on our hustle," Keebler said with a smile, but Big Dee was thinking differently. Once he got ahold to another brick and Twin came around to buy it, he would serve the man. The way he saw it, Keebler and Krash could pick who they wanted to serve because they had the money and dope on deck. Big Dee knew he didn't have that luxury, and if he wanted to come up in the game, he had to take chances.

"I do need another chicken," Big Dee said suddenly as he passed the ten grand to Keebler.

"How soon do you need it?" Keebler asked.

***

"What's on your mind, cuz?" Dirty asked after he rolled a blunt. Twin had not said a word since they pulled off, so he knew his cousin had something on his mind. Twin decided to keep it real with his cousin since he was known in the streets for putting in work. For all he knew, Dirty probably knew something about the murders.

"Check this out," Twin said and gave his cousin the brown paper bag. Dirty pulled out the kilo and immediately recognized the logo from the brick he'd given his cousin the day before.

"What's wrong with it?" he asked.

"That logo is from my big homie," Twin said as he fought back the tears in his eyes. He had to pull over at a gas station because his vision began to blur. Dirty just stared at his cousin because he didn't understand what was going on.

"My nigga was killed a couple of days ago," Twin said as he wiped his face.

All of a sudden, Dirty understood, and he found himself getting mad. If what his cousin was hinting at was true, then he'd been used in the whole scheme of things.

"You don't think my niggas had something to do with that, do you?" Dirty asked, but he already knew the answer because he was down with them.

"Somebody within that group know something, and whoever participated in the murder have to answer to my homies," Twin said, getting mad as he thought about the scene he remembered seeing the day of the murder.

So much was going on in Dirty's mind, so he lit the blunt he was holding and took three hard pulls. "Let me find out what's going on before you start a war that may just be bigger than you," Dirty suggested.

The comment made Twin laugh because as far as he was concerned, they were just two old heads who overstepped their boundaries in the streets. Who were they against a group of gangsters ready to defend the honor of one of their homeboys?

"I can't stop you from looking out for your homeboys, but me and my homies are about to take matters into our own hands," Twin told his cousin as he took the blunt. He pulled back into traffic without waiting for a reply because in his mind, he was about to avenge his big homie's death.

For the rest of the ride back to North Memphis, Dirty didn't say anything. They just passed the blunt back and forth while he tried to figure out a way to stop a war that could possibly have him going against his own family.

***

Now back in traffic, Keebler was trying to figure out how to tell his best friend that they may have fucked up.

"What's going on?" Krash asked as he snorted more cocaine. Keebler just smiled as he drove, then decided to put it all on the table.

"When we hit dude in North Memphis, did you notice the logo he had on his dope?" Keebler asked.

"Tank always put a tank symbol on his work to let his customers know whose dope it was," Krash said without thinking about it.

"The first brick we sold to Twin had the logo on it, as did the second. With dude being from North Memphis, I think he somehow connected to dude," Keebler explained.

"Ain't dude some kin to Dirty?" Krash asked.

"Yep," Keebler replied.

"Well, wouldn't he let us know if his cousin suspected us?" Krash asked, trying to get an understanding of how serious the subject was.

"He can't inform us of something he's not aware of," Keebler said.

It was as if the last comment put all the pieces of the puzzle together for Krash because he looked at his best friend with an expression that said murder was the answer.

"Before we react, let's at least see what Dirty knows. We owe him that much respect before we have to put him in a awkward position," Krash suggested.

"I'm already on it," Keebler replied as he dialed numbers on his phone. The voice he was looking for answered on the third ring.

***

When Twin pulled back up in the hood, he parked at the curb so his cousin could leave in his car.

"Let me get some of that weed," he said with a slur. Dirty looked at his cousin, and then they both started laughing for no apparent reason.

"You know I got you, kinfolk," he said and went into the Ziploc bag. Twin noticed for the first time that the weed was something he'd never had.

"Let me check into that situation before you make any moves," Dirty said as he passed his cousin a handful of buds.

"Handle your business," Twin replied as he put the weed inside the brown paper bag the kilo was in.

As far as he was concerned, that whole group played some part in the assassination of his big homie. He just had to prove it some way, and he had an idea how he could, but this was something he had to keep from his cousin.

Dirty was just getting in his Beamer when his phone rang.

"What you know, big bruh?" Dirty answered once he was in the car.

"Where you at?" Keebler asked.

"I'm out north about to head your way. We need to talk," Dirty said as a matter of fact.

"I have a feeling I know what about. Where do you wanna meet at?" Keebler asked.

"Shit, I'm in traffic right now. I wanted to go back and kick it with Flea, but I can be wherever you wanna meet up at," Dirty said as he continued to head back to the southside. Since they had to take Big Dee another kilo, Keebler decided to make that the meeting spot. Plus, he knew Flea would warn him if they were walking into a trap.

"I'll meet you on the block in a few," Keebler said and ended the call.

As Dirty headed back to South Memphis, he didn't know what the future held, but he knew there was about to be drama in the streets.

For some reason, Keebler ended the call already anticipating going to war with some gangbangers, and that was the last thing he wanted. He took two piles of powder up each nostril to help him figure out how to deal with the situation at hand.

"How do you wanna approach this?" Keebler asked Krash suddenly.

"What do you mean?" Krash asked back. Keebler explained as best as he could what he was feeling, but the truth of the matter was the cocaine had his emotions running wild.

"We both know what type of dude Dirty is because he got most of his game from us," Keebler said. "The question is, do we need to consider him as a enemy?" he asked.

"I have no doubt that Dirty is loyal to us, but if it will make you feel better, we can double up on pistols," Krash replied without hesitation.

"You know I keep the twins on me anyways," Keebler said before lifting his shirt to show the two Glock .40s he was accustomed to carrying.

***

A call came through that required Flea to have to ride across town to make a serve, so he asked his best friend to ride with him.

"I have to pass this time. If you gone, that means I can get some of that good weed money that you be getting," Big Dee said honestly.

Flea had sold him a pound of that new weed, and to hear that he wanted to stay back and paperchase surprised him. "Hold down the fort until I get back," Flea said, giving the man dap before strutting off to his car that was parked on the curb.

Big Dee watched his best friend leave then immediately got back on his hustle. Not five minutes had passed when Dirty came speeding up the block.

At first, Big Dee didn't know what to do. Then he remembered what Flea told him about being part of the family. With a smile, he walked over to where the young hitman was parking.

"Where Flea?" Dirty jumped out and asked.

"He had a serve to go make," Big Dee replied. Even though he felt safe, a part of him still watched every move Dirty made.

The two men held small conversations, trying to feel each other out until they both got comfortable with each other. By the time Keebler pulled back up, Big Dee and Dirty were sitting under the tint of the BMW smoking blunts.

***

About an hour after Dirty left the house, Midnight found herself unable to sleep. For some reason, she couldn't get Flea out of her head. She was starting to fall for the man, and she knew he was feeling her.

"I have to do this," she told herself as she got up for the day.

The first thing she did was roll a blunt of Hydro that she had been holding on to. As she scrolled through the contacts in her phone, Midnight found the number she was looking for. After pressing Send on the phone, she patiently waited for someone to pick up while she lit the blunt. The sweet smell of the weed as it went up her nostrils and entered her brain seemed to turn her on.

"Hello," a feminine voice answered on the third ring.

***

After Keebler and Krash made it back to the house, they pulled up just as Trina and Zya were about to leave.

"Where you ladies headed?" Keebler asked as he hopped out the car.

"I have a few things that I need, so we decided to go get them while you boys hustled," Zya said in a seductive voice.

"Do you need some money?" Keebler asked, but they both went in their pockets and pulled out bankrolls. Without waiting on a reply, Keebler gave Zya his half of the ten grand he'd made from the brick serve in South Memphis.

"You girls be careful," Krash spoke up as Trina hopped behind the wheel of his Crown Vic.

"We will," both girls replied at the same time. The men both stood back and watched as they backed out of the driveway and sped off up the street.

"You know they up to something, don't you?" Krash said as they went in the house.

"Yep," Keebler said like he couldn't have cared less. "Let the girls be girls. Right now, we got other shit to worry about," he continued once they were in the office where the dope was stashed.

Keebler told Krash to grab two kilos instead of one. "The way that young nigga is chasing that paper, he'll be needing another one in a day or so," he said.

"Say no more," Krash said as he did what Keebler asked.

They quickly checked their pistols to make sure they had protection in case something popped off, and then they headed right back out the door. Keebler got back behind the wheel, then pulled out his dollar bill that was now almost empty.

"Fill me back up before we pull off," he suggested.

Krash pulled out the sandwich bag and took out three chunks of cocaine. "Break it down yourself. I gotta get myself right," Krash said as he put the dope in his best friend's dollar bill. He put some more powder in his own dollar bill and crushed it before they both stuffed their noses. Once they got their drain, Keebler headed back to the southside to meet up with Dirty.

***

As Trina cruised through the afternoon traffic with the system bumping, it dawned on her that it had been a while since she'd had a girls day out. She glanced over at Zya, who was leaning back in the passenger seat with a huge smile on her face.

"What got you over there smiling so much?" Trina muted the system and asked.

"Girl, I'm so high! I got all types of shit going on in here," Zya replied while she pointed to her head.

"Does it have anything to do with where we going?" Trina asked. The look Zya gave her was all the confirmation she needed.

"On some more shit, it's been a long time since I had some female friends to kick shit with," Zya admitted.

"Girl, it's been a while for me too," Trina replied. Just like that, the girls had something to talk about as they headed across town.

***

Once Midnight ended her call, she finished smoking on her blunt, then took a quick shower. After she got dressed, she was about to roll up another blunt until the sound of bass was heard. Looking out the window, Midnight smiled when she saw Trina had driven the Crown Vic to pick her up. Without wasting any time, she locked up the house and strutted to the car where her only friends in the world were waiting.

"What's up, bitches?" Midnight hopped in the backseat and greeted.

"Your nasty ass," Zya replied, and the girls all laughed.

"Pull on off before Dirty pull up," Midnight said as she got comfortable in the back seat. Trina pulled off, and Zya began rolling another blunt until Midnight stopped her.

"Roll this shit here up," she said and passed her the sandwich bag with Hydro in it. Trina glanced over at the weed and just shook her head.

"I hope you know what you doing," Trina said as she continued driving.

"I do as long as I know I can count on y'all to have my back," Midnight said like a little girl.

"You know we got you," Zya said.

"Just handle your business and call me to pick you up before we all get in trouble," Trina said.

Midnight got on the phone and called Flea. Instead of saying who she was, she pretended to be a customer wanting to buy some Hydro. The meeting spot was at the Hampton Inn on Perkins Road, and Flea said he would call back once he was in the area. Midnight ended the call to find Zya holding the blunt she'd just rolled and watching her.

"I just got one question. How did you get that boy number?" she asked as she lit the blunt.

"It was on the cover of his CD," Midnight admitted sheepishly. She explained how bad she wanted to fuck Flea and couldn't think of anything else until she quenched her thirst. While they headed to the hotel, they got high and got the plan together so they'd have the same story in the future.

***

When Keebler swerved up on the block in South Memphis, they were so high and paranoid that he almost kept driving past the Beamer parked at the curb. Nothing seemed out of the ordinary to the men, so they both hopped out with their pistols showing on their waistlines. As Dirty and Big Dee got out the BMW, they both had smiles on their faces.

"What's up with that?" Dirty asked, immediately noticing a difference in the men he looked at as big brothers.

"What you talking about?" Keebler asked as he watched the young killer's every move.

Little did they know, the way they were now acting let Dirty know they were the ones behind the death of whoever his cousin spoke about. He only hoped they didn't think he was down with the gangbangers.

"Y'all got your pistols ready for easy access like you're anticipating something," Dirty said to let the men know he was hip to the move. "We both know why I asked to meet up, but I hope you don't think I'd go against y'all," he continued while looking both of them in the eyes.

"What about your cousin?" Krash asked.

Dirty explained that Twin suspected they were behind the death of a big homie, but he didn't know for sure. "I told him I'd get at y'all, but the last thing I want is my cousin to beef with my niggas," Dirty explained. "I love Twin, but I'll kill about you old heads, so if I have a say in this, you know nothing about no murders," he continued.

"That's what's up, but you should know that if he come at us at any angle but the right one, you will have a decision to make because I'll off him," Keebler stated firmly as he gave Dirty a hug.

13

When Flea pulled onto the lot at the Hampton Inn, he texted the number that had last called to get the room number. As he found a parking space close to the entrance, he received the text he was looking for. As he checked out his surroundings before hopping out the Crown Vic, Flea didn't see anything out of the ordinary, so he went on in the establishment. The room number was 104, which was on the first floor, so he headed to the room and knocked on the door. Flea knew it was a female who wanted the weed, but he was not ready for what he saw when the door opened.

Midnight stood in the door in a bowlegged stance with nothing but a black bra and panty set on and a look in her eyes that instantly made Flea's dick hard.

"You gone stand out there or come get some of this chocolate?" Midnight asked seductively. As a reply, Flea stepped in the room and closed the door, then immediately got naked. He didn't know what Midnight had planned, but he was ready to dive in and go to work.

"We don't have long, so make it count," she whispered in his ear as he laid her down on the bed. He had to take a moment and just look at her body before they got down to do the nasty.

"Put that dick in me now!" Midnight demanded, and Flea was happy to oblige.

He could feel the heat coming from her body as he led his nine inches into her treasure chest.

"Ooh, baby!" Midnight moaned as she moved her hips so she could get all of him inside her.

Flea started going in and out of that pussy, moving slow at first. With each stroke, he sped up the pace with Midnight matching his every stroke with a turn of her hips. Flea felt like he'd died and gone to heaven, and he found himself thinking about other things to prolong the fucking he was putting on her. When Midnight started clawing at his back, he knew she was ready to burst.

"Turn over and let me hit that ass from the back!" Flea said as he suddenly pulled out of her. His dick was soaking wet with her juices, and when Midnight saw this, she surprised him by putting his dick in her mouth. Flea just closed his eyes and enjoyed the way her mouth felt. Once she had sucked him clean again, she bent over and put that pussy in his face.

When Flea saw the juices sliding out of that pretty pink pussy, he knelt down and took a lick. Midnight hadn't been expecting to feel any tongue, so when she felt his against her dripping pussy, she started purring like a kitten.

For the next five minutes Flea sucked on her pussy like it was his last meal. When he finally did stick his dick back inside of her, they both were ready to release the pressure that had built inside of them. Flea hit her with some long, hard strokes, listening to the sounds her pussy made as she got wetter.

"I'm cumming!" Midnight yelled as they both climaxed together before falling out on the bed. Without knowing it, they both went straight to sleep.

***

Twin tried to get about his hustle, but his mind kept going back to the day the big homie was killed. There was no doubt in his mind that Keebler and Krash were somehow involved. He just couldn't prove it. For the rest of the day, he went back and forth over whether he should push on the men or wait until Dirty checked out the facts. By the time the sun was starting to set, Twin came up with a plan that would help him keep his word to his cousin and allow him to avenge Tank's death at the same time.

After making a few more serves, Twin called it a night and closed up the traphouse. As he sped off the block, he called his brother Ya-Yo.

"What's good?" Ya-Yo asked on the second ring.

"How soon can you get some wheels to do some dirt in?" Twin asked as he sped up Chelsea.

"It's some young niggas out here right now burning up the block in some steamers," Ya-Yo replied.

Twin could hear what sounded like multiple vehicles burning rubber in the background. "Snatch one of them up, and I'll be at you in about five," he said and ended the call without waiting for a reply.

***

Since Flea was still missing from the block, Big Dee got about his hustle. He was making money from both the weed he'd got and the powder from the two kilos he'd gotten when Keebler met up with Dirty. They'd sat around and smoked on blunts after the meeting, but as the day began to end, Keebler and Krash left, saying they had some business to handle.

An hour later, Dirty decided to call it a day since Flea still hadn't made it back to the hood yet.

***

When Twin pulled up on the scene, he found Ya-Yo sitting on the hood of a blue Dodge Challenger.

"I hope this will do for whatever you got planned," Ya-Yo said as soon as Twin hopped out the Cutlass.

"What *we* got planned. Let's ride out," Twin said, already hopping in the passenger seat of the stolen car. Ya-Yo hopped behind the wheel and pulled off without saying a word because he knew his brother would eventually fill him in on what was going on.

"Head to South Memphis. I got something to handle," Twin said suddenly as he rolled up a blunt. He gave the street name they were headed to and let Ya-Yo know what he had up his sleeve.

"It looks like I grabbed the right car since we'll be in and out," Ya-Yo replied as he hopped on the interstate. He could've taken several backstreets to get to where they were going, but he wanted to let the HEMI loose, and the best place to do that was on an open stretch. Plus, he wanted to avoid the police as much as possible.

****

"So, where to now?" Krash asked Keebler as they sped away from the block.

"I figured while we were already in the area, we may as well scope out our next victim," Keebler said with a smile.

"Say no more," Krash replied, then put a couple of scoops of cocaine in his nose.

When they finally did pull up on the block of their next robbery, Krash immediately noticed that the lay-out was a lot more complicated than the area where they robbed Tank.

"I don't see no easy way of getting to the house without confrontation," Krash said as he continued scoping out the area.

"We'll have to go in like we wanna actually buy some work. Then, when they show us the merchandise, we'll do what we do," Keebler explained.

"Kill everything not with us?" Krash asked hesitantly.

"Have I ever spared a motherfucker?" Keebler replied with a smile as his answer. He pointed to where they would park, then drove to where the second vehicle would be.

***

It didn't take Ya-Yo much time to get to the hood Twin told him to drive to. As he pulled up on the block, Twin found what he was looking for.

"Ride down on dude getting out that car," he said as he nodded to where Big Dee was.

Ya-Yo pulled down on the hustler as Twin rolled his window down. When Big Dee saw who it was in the Challenger, Keebler's words went through his mind, but he never had a chance to react. Before the car had completely stopped, Twin was already hopping out.

Boc! Boc! Boc! Boc!

All four shots hit Big Dee in his chest, knocking him to the sidewalk. Thinking the man was dead, Twin went in his pockets and took all of his money.

"Your homeboys will see you in hell shortly," he said and spit on the man before quickly retreating to the car. Ya-Yo sped off, leaving nothing but smoke in the air behind them.

***

Back at the Hampton Inn, Midnight was awakened by the sound of her phone ringing. Laying beside her still sleep was Flea, and she couldn't help but smile as she answered the phone.

"Bitch! We outside waiting on you," Trina said before Midnight spoke.

"My bad, girl. I'm on the way out now," Midnight said and ended the call just as Flea was starting to wake up.

"You leaving before round two?" he asked as he watched her get dressed.

"I have to go, but we'll do this again real soon," Midnight promised.

As good as she was looking to Flea, when his phone started ringing, he turned straight into hustler mode.

"What's up?" he answered on the second ring. As he listened to what was being said, a look of terror appeared on his face as he jumped out of bed. "I'm on the way now," Flea said and ended the call to find Midnight looking at him strangely.

Instead of heading back to the block, Flea headed downtown to Regional One Hospital where the caller said Big Dee had been taken. As he pulled up, he knew he was at the right spot because most of the hustlers from the hood were standing out front with confused looks on their faces. Flea found a parking spot and put some money in the meter before speed-walking to the hospital.

"What happened?" Flea asked the first familiar face he stepped up to.

"Big Dee got robbed and shot in the chest four times," a hustler spoke up.

After hearing that his best friend had been shot that many times, Flea knew he was dead, but he needed confirmation. "Is he dead?" Flea asked.

"He was alive when we got here. He in emergency surgery right now," the hustler explained.

Hearing his best friend was still alive put the young dopeboy at ease a bit, but he knew it was no coincidence that Big Dee was targeted. He stepped away from everybody else as he pulled out his phone and made a call.

***

Just as they agreed on how the next lick would go, Keebler's phone started ringing. "Flea finally back on the radar," he said as he recognized the number. "What up, young nigga?" he answered on the third ring.

"Did you have something to do with Big Dee getting shot up?" Flea asked.

"What?!" Keebler said. "What happened?" he asked back, then listened as Flea explained everything that was told to him. As Keebler listened, Dirty immediately came to mind. "I promise I didn't have a hand in that shit," Keebler said. "Where you at now?" he asked.

"I'm at Regional One waiting on Big Dee to come out of surgery," Flea said.

"We on the way to you now," Keebler said and ended the call to find Krash watching him. "Somebody popped Big Dee on the track," Keebler said as he dialed numbers on his phone.

"You don't think lil bruh had a hand in that, do you?" Krash asked, already thinking what Keebler was thinking.

***

Dirty had just pulled up at the crib when he got a call. Looking at the number, he got a bad vibe.

"What up?" he slowly answered.

"Where you at, young nigga?" Keebler asked.

"At the crib about to take a shower," Dirty stated as he went in the house.

"Please tell me you didn't have nothing to do with Big Dee getting shot," Keebler said.

The question caught Dirty by surprise, and he had to sit down. "Big bruh, when I left the south, the young nigga was getting about his hustle," he pleaded.

Keebler explained what he knew about the robbery and said they were on the way to the hospital to check on him.

"So, he's alive?" Dirty asked.

"As far as we know. He took four to the chest and had to have emergency surgery," Keebler said.

"Four to the chest! Somebody was really trying to kill him," Dirty said out loud, but he was talking to himself. Keebler heard the comment and immediately put two and two together.

"We'll be at Regional One if you find anything out," Keebler said, ready to hang up.

"Let me take a quick shower, and I'll meet y'all up there," Dirty said and ended the call.

"I think I know who shot my young nigga," Keebler told his best friend after he ended the call with Dirty.

"If it wasn't lil bruh, I'm guessing it was probably his kinfolk," Krash said, ready to put in some work.

"We all thinking the same thing. I say we let bruh find out what's up before we push," Keebler explained. Krash agreed to fall back for the moment, but both men had already made it up in their minds what needed to be done. Until the time presented itself, they would focus on helping Big Dee get back healthy enough to hustle.

***

The adrenaline rush Twin felt after putting in that work was overwhelming.

"That's for Tank," he said out loud as he split the money he'd gotten off Big Dee with his brother Ya-Yo.

"This is what I call a day's work," Ya-Yo said while holding his portion of the money up by the rearview mirror.

"Is there any way we can keep this car?" Twin asked. "We'll need it when we put in more work," he continued before Ya-Yo could speak.

"The hood is too hot right now to stash anything," Ya-Yo replied.

"I know a spot that's safe if we can make it to Scutterfield after we pick up my car," Twin said after thinking about it.

"I'll just follow you to the hood," Ya-Yo replied just as they were pulling up behind the Cutlass.

"Head on to the hood now, and I'll meet you at the trap," Twin said as he hopped out the Challenger.

Instead of replying, Ya-Yo sped off, causing the sports car to go up the street sideways and leave a cloud of smoke on the block. Twin just shook his head, laughing until he got a text message.

***

Instead of calling Twin to warn him and have a long debate, Dirty just sent him a text, then went to take a shower. After he got out, he noticed Midnight was gone. He called her and put the phone on speaker so he could get dressed.

"Hello," Midnight answered.

"What's up, baby? Where you at?" Dirty asked.

"Riding around with Trina and Zya," Midnight answered. "We having a girls day out," she continued her story.

"Oh. Well, I'm about to jump back in the streets and ride up to Regional One," Dirty explained.

"For what?" Midnight asked. Without giving too many details over the phone, Dirty explained that Big Dee had been shot.

"Where's big bruh?" Midnight asked since she knew Keebler had taken Big Dee under his wing.

"They meeting me up there," Dirty replied.

"We'll meet you there as well. That way, I can hop in the car with you," Midnight suggested.

Dirty agreed and ended the call just as he finished getting dressed, then headed out the door.

They all met up at Regional One Hospital just minutes after each other. Keebler couldn't have cared less about finding a parking spot and just double parked in front of the hospital, where Flea and other hustlers from the hood were standing out. Before everyone could get acquainted, Dirty pulled up and parked behind the Crown Vic. Just as he was hopping out, Trina came swerving around the corner with the system blasting. Everyone who was standing outside knew who the car belonged to. What they didn't expect was the three sexy women who hopped out the custom ride. Krash heard someone swear under their breath as they all checked out the women, and it made him smile. Everybody watched as each woman went to her man, but it was Keebler who caught the seductive glance between Flea and Midnight.

"How is Big Dee doing, baby?" Zya asked Keebler.

"He's still in surgery right now. For the time being, all we can do is wait," Keebler replied.

For the next couple of hours, they all stood outside waiting to see what the doctors would be able to do. An elderly lady, who they would find out later that she was Big Dee's grandma and only relative still alive, slowly walked out and eased up to Flea. Nobody but Flea could hear what the woman was saying, but they all knew she was giving good news when Flea showed his infamous smile that always got the girls' attention.

"I'll be back, y'all. My guy is requesting to see me," Flea told the crowd.

"You let Big Dee know we out here rooting for him," Keebler spoke, but his eyes told another story. Flea caught the eye contact and nodded before helping Big Dee's grandma back in the hospital.

"Who do you think did that shit, big bruh?" Dirty asked suddenly.

"I don't know," Keebler said softly.

***

When Twin got back to the hood, he had to read the unbelievable text again. Ya-Yo walked up and hopped in the passenger seat as he was reading the text, so without a word, Twin passed the phone so he could see what he was looking at.

"Who sent this?" Ya-Yo asked.

"My cousin," Twin replied softly.

"This can't be true. You hit that bitch at point blank range," Ya-Yo said in disbelief.

"What does the text say, bruh?" Twin asked.

"If you had anything to do with the shooting in South Memphis, you need to know that he didn't die," Ya-Yo read the text out loud like it would somehow change the message. "Did you reply back?" he asked suddenly.

Twin just shook his head. He had a lot on his plate at the moment, and he was trying to figure out the best way to deal with the issue. Both men got quiet for a few minutes.

"Until I figure out how to deal with this, I want you to stay in the hood and try to stay off the radar," Twin explained. In his eyes, there was only one way to deal with everything, and that was to finish what he started.

"Say no more," Ya-Yo said. Twin jumped out the car and went to the trap to get some weed for them to smoke. When he came back out, he found Ya-Yo listening to the sound system in the Cutlass.

***

Dirty was trying to stick around to see what Big Dee had to say about whoever robbed and shot him, but Midnight was ready to go home.

"Let me get at bruh right quick, and then we can leave," he said, then walked over to where Keebler and Krash were. "Baby ready to call it a day, so we about to dip, but let me know the outcome of everything," Dirty told the men.

"You may not like the outcome or the aftermath, but if you really wanna know, we got you," Krash spoke up.

"Just know that whatever the aftermath may be, I'm on your side," Dirty said, reading between the lines. He gave both men dap, then walked off with Midnight following.

"I think he suspect the same person we do," Keebler said as they watched Dirty hop in his BMW and speed off.

"It's in his eyes," Krash stated. "And it's eating him up to know what's about to happen. I can tell he wants to help put a stop to it," he continued. "And because of that, we need to pay close attention to his movements," Krash said low enough for only the two of them to hear.

An hour later, Flea came back out of the hospital with a look in his eyes that neither Keebler nor Krash had ever seen before.

"What's the word, young nigga?" Keebler asked, already knowing what was about to be said.

"Big Dee said the cat Dirty brought to the hood earlier and got the brick rode back through and robbed him," Flea said.

"We had already suspected him," Krash explained. "He think we got something to do with some gangbanging shit that happened in North Memphis," he continued.

"That's probably why he left a foul message for y'all," Flea said.

"What message is that?" Keebler asked.

"He told my guy not to worry because y'all will be joining him in hell shortly," Flea replied. The threat made the men laugh to keep from exposing the anger they really felt at the moment.

"Do you know anyone you trust who'll wanna make some good bread by staying here at the hospital with Big Dee?" Keebler asked.

"I know a few niggas looking for a chance to get down with some real niggas," Flea answered. Before Keebler could reply, he dipped off to a group of teenagers from his hood who were just lounging around. He came back with a young man who looked like he really grew up in the struggle. "Big homies, this is my lil' nigga Twoine. I use him to keep a watch on my trap," Flea explained.

***

"Where'd you get the weed from?" Ya-Yo asked after they'd finished blowing on the second blunt.

"My cousin bought this shit from South Memphis," Twin said as he reclined in his seat.

"That shit is smoking, bruh. I'm high as shit," Ya-Yo said and laughed for no reason.

Twin looked over the man and laughed with him, even though neither person had said anything funny. Twin ended up talking Ya-Yo into chilling in Scutterfield with him for the rest of the night, and they both went to the trap so Twin could get about his hustle.

***

"Do you know who we are?" Keebler asked the youngster Flea had just brought into their circle.

"No, but I take it y'all some real niggas if Flea fuck with y'all as tough as he do," Twoine replied.

"I aint trying to talk down on you or no shit like that, but you look like you could use a few dollars to upgrade your game," Krash spoke up. His voice was known to intimidate people from its bass, and he was trying to see how the youngster would react.

"I'm always looking for a hustle," Twoine replied, never losing his composure.

"How much will you charge me to stay up here with Big Dee? I'm talking about making sure nobody but us and his family is able to get close to him," Keebler explained. He could tell the question caught him by surprise because he looked over at Flea for confirmation that the old heads were serious.

"You know the reason I'm up here to begin with is because Big Dee is my homeboy. I'll keep an eye on him for you, and you just fuck with me how you see fit," Twoine replied. Little did he know, Krash was really feeling his demeanor and was thinking about taking him under his wing after everything was over.

"Keep my nigga safe, and we got you," Keebler promised.

"That's what's up," Twoine said before giving the men dap.

***

When Dirty finally made it home, he was glad that Midnight wasn't in the mood for sex because he had a lot on his mind. He still hadn't heard back from his cousin about the text he sent, and that was making him look guilty in his eyes. He was also thinking about the retaliation that was about to take place. There was no doubt in his mind that Keebler and Krash would find out who shot Big Dee. They would bring a war to whoever violated someone they considered family, and it didn't matter if they were affiliated. Getting down in the streets was what they did, and they were very good at their hustle. As much as he hated to admit it, this was one time he couldn't choose sides, and the only way to make sure he stayed neutral was to make sure he wasn't around when the shit hit the fan. After hours of contemplating, he decided it was time he took a long vacation. By the time he finally went to sleep, the sun was about to rise.

***

Once Keebler and Krash knew they had Big Dee secured, they decided to call it a night. Krash insisted that they follow him to his house to spend the night. Keebler agreed but only under the condition that they would stop and pick up a couple of steamers for the mission they had to complete the next day. It didn't take long to find the vehicles he was looking for. While the girls drove both Crown Vics, Keebler and Krash drove the stolen cars to the spots where they usually stashed vehicles before jumping back in their own cars. They all headed to Coro Lake and surprisingly went straight to bed.

***

After the big homies left the hospital, Flea had a long talk with Twoine.

"You know you about to come up in the game, don't it?" Flea asked.

"Why you say that?" Twoine asked.

"Who you think put Big Dee on?" Flea asked. "They had some work to get off and asked me if I had someone who'd wanna get some paper," he continued.

"Besides they cars, they don't look much like dopeboys," Twoine replied.

"They not," Flea said, smiling. From the look Twoine had on his face, he knew he was confused, so Flea broke the game down to him. This was his way of explaining how critical it was that he kept his word about looking out for Big Dee.

"It's about to be a lot of shit going on in these streets, homie, and it's always best to have niggas like that on your side," Flea replied. "As long as you don't let nothing happen to Big Dee, when he comes home, there's a good chance you may get a brick or two plus some bread for your services. Not to mention you'll be a part of our crew, nigga," Flea explained.

Hearing this put a huge smile on Twoine's face because he'd always wanted to be part of something, but most people looked down on him because he wasn't able to afford the designer clothes and shoes the other hustlers had.

"I'll put my life on the line to make sure Big Dee get better," Twoine promised, then gave Flea dap.

14

Out in East Memphis, another hunt was going on, and this time, Keebler was the hunted. The men who got caught up with Godzilla at the courts were members of the Black Gorilla Cartel, a crew of killers from Miami who sent drugs to most of the East Coast. They were Shorty Bud's new plug, and they sent some men to Memphis to find out more about their future clients. Now, more members of the BGC were in the city with a hit squad ready to avenge their fallen brothers. One of the big men had gotten possession of Godzilla's phone and after going through it, they came across the photo of Keebler with the text "Dead Man Walking" under it. They didn't know if the face in the phone had anything to do with the shooting, but if he did, they had people in place to deal with the issue.

***

On the other side of town, Keebler and Krash were getting ready to put in some more work.

"I know we said we'd pull up at the target in this SS Impala, but I say we switch the cars around and use this pretty muthafucka as the second ride. That way, once we drop the work off, we can ride through North Memphis and start some real shit," Keebler suggested.

Krash glanced from the new SS Impala to the Mustang GT and had to admit that even he liked the idea. "That's cool. Let's just go get this paper," Krash said as he hopped in the GT.

The spot they were headed to was where the old Lamar Terrace projects once stood. They had been torn down and replaced with middle-class townhomes, but the drug money was still around. One of the townhomes was run by a dopeboy named Face. Although he only purchased five kilos a month, his traphouse made most of its profits from selling rock for rock. This caused his name to ring in the city's underground.

Knowing this, Face had men on his payroll to ensure business stayed business. Buford always watched the door while Torren stayed at Face's side while he conducted his business. As thought-out as the set up was, none of the men anticipated that robbers were planning to kill them and everyone else who tried to stop them.

Once they reached the switch-point, Keebler made sure to park the Impala in a spot where they didn't have to worry about police finding the car beforehand. As soon as he jumped in the GT, Krash headed to their target. The scene wasn't nearly as live as it had been the day before, and Krash was glad. He didn't have a problem blowing somebody's brains out of their head. He just didn't want more people to die than the lick called for, and it looked like his wish had been answered again.

"Just pull up at the trap. This ain't our shit, so it won't matter if somebody get the tag numbers," Keebler said as they pulled up at the townhomes.

"I got this, nigga. You just remember: we go in there like real dopeboys. That means wait until we see the medicine before we push," Krash replied just as he was parking in front of the traphouse. Since they knew they were being watched, they hopped out the car and strutted up to the door, where they were immediately met by Buford.

"Face around?" Krash asked.

"Who wants to know?" Buford asked, getting a bad vibe from the men in front of him.

"Let him know money at the door," Keebler spoke up. As far as he was concerned, the door was open, so the opportunity was there.

Krash felt what was about to happen, so he sprang into action. In one swift movement, he came up with two P-95 Ruger Glocks and hit Buford in the head with the butt of one gun before putting the barrel of the other in his mouth when he tried to scream. Keebler pushed the man back in the house, then rushed in behind him to find Face and another man in the dining room sitting at a table. On the table were three kilos and a pile of money.

"Shit, looks like we right on time for the party," Keebler said as he eased up with his two Glocks pointed at each man. Krash had Buford secured with a Glock at his head. The man's mouth was bloody from having the pistol shoved in his mouth, and the sight was frightening.

Torren jumped up like he could beat Keebler to the punch but got a rude awakening.

Boc! Boc!

Torren was dead before his body hit the floor.

Boc!

Krash gave Buford a head shot to show Face they meant business.

"That was just to show you we ain't playing," Keebler said as he nodded at the dead bodies while never taking his eyes off the man. "You already know what this is, so the outcome of it depends on whether you play ball," he continued as he stepped up to the table. Krash knew Keebler would handle business, so he just stayed at the front door in case somebody tried to help Face.

"Take that shit. I don't want no problems," Face said while crossing his arms like he was pouting.

Keebler stared at the man for a minute, trying to see if he was trying them. Then, without warning, he closed the distance until he was standing in front of him with both Glocks aimed at the man's forehead. He leaned in close so only Face could hear him.

"If I search this place and find anything, you'll see another side of me," Keebler whispered.

"I got a floor safe that's already open in the bedroom closet. The rest of the dope and money is in it," Face gave in.

Krash checked outside one more time to make sure everything was good, then ran to the bedroom to check the safe. He stepped out minutes later carrying a duffelbag. He eased up to the table and put the rest of the work with everything else before nodding to Keebler. With a smile on his face, Keebler started backing away from Face as if he would spare his life. Once he was certain Face thought he would live, the smile disappeared.

Boc! Boc! Boc! Boc!

Face took four shots to his torso and slid out of his chair. To make sure they wouldn't have an episode like the one Big Dee had, he went back over to the two bodies and kicked.

Boc! Boc!

A shot to each man's head ensured that they joined Buford in hell. Then they casually walked out the townhome like nothing happened. They hopped in the GT and pulled off with ease, and as soon as they were back in traffic, Krash headed to the other car.

"That trick had almost thirty bricks in the safe and at least a hundred racks," Krash said suddenly.

"For real?" Keebler asked in disbelief. He thought the man had around ten bricks at the most. Either way, he was one less man to have to worry about competing with.

When they got to the SS Impala, Keebler jumped behind the wheel and headed back toward Coro Lake.

"I wanna make a point when we go out north," Keebler said as they cruised down the interstate.

"You wanna pull the big guns out, dont it?" Krash asked a question he already knew the answer to.

Keebler could only smile as he thought about what they were about to do. "I know just the rifle I'm using too," he said, sounding like a little kid.

They made it to the house with no problems and found the girls smoking weed and barbecuing in the backyard. They went to put up the dope and money before loading up two .223 assault rifles with the same type of one hundred round drums they would put on the AK-47s.

"Them niggas ain't gone be ready for this," Krash said as he checked to make sure his rifle was in working order.

"That young nigga rode through the south with no regard for Big Dee's life. It's only right that we return the favor," Keebler said.

"We don't know where he dwell at," Krash said.

Keebler thought about it and realized his best friend was right. "You think Midnight know?" he asked.

Trina and Zya were sitting back enjoying the breeze coming from the lake while they smoked on blunts and barbecued when Keebler led the way outside.

"I see y'all got it going on," he said while nodding his head to Marvin Gaye. He knelt down and gave Zya a light but passionate kiss before turning his attention to Trina. "I need a big favor from you, sis," Keebler said, sounding like a kid again.

"What is it, boy?" Trina asked, sounding like a big sister.

"We need you ladies to find out where Dirty cousin Twin hang out at," Keebler explained.

"How am I supposed to do that?" Trina asked.

"How about you go pick up Midnight and bring her to the house since y'all have become good friends?" Krash spoke up.

"Yeah! Just call her up and tell her y'all coming to get her," Keebler said. "Please, sis. This is very important," Keebler asked.

Trina looked over at Zya with a smile. "Alright," she said, then pulled out her phone to call Midnight.

"While you ladies go do that, we got some more business to handle. We'll be back in a few," Krash said, then led the way through the house to where the rifles were. They both grabbed their guns and headed out the door.

When Midnight woke up to answer the phone, she noticed Dirty had already left. Beside the bed on the nightstand was a letter.

"Hello," Midnight answered the call as she got up.

"You still sleep, girl? Flea must've wore that ass out," Trina said, making both women laugh.

"I don't know what happened, girl," Midnight replied as she picked up the letter.

"I was calling to see if you wanted to come to the crib and chill with us. Me and Zya barbecuing and getting high," Trina said.

For a moment, Midnight didn't reply because she was reading the letter still. "Shit, I may as well. My dumb-ass nigga done went out of town, and instead of telling me, he left a note," Midnight said, getting mad.

Hearing that, Trina decided to press her luck. "Do you think his cousin Twin went with him?" she asked.

"Twin young ass is not leaving Scutterfield. He is strictly a dopeboy," Midnight explained.

"Well, get your ass up 'cause we on the way to you now," Trina said, happy that she got the information she was looking for. Midnight agreed to be ready and ended the call.

"That wasn't hard at all," Trina told Zya as she called her man.

"What exactly do our men do anyways?" Zya asked.

Trina told her to wait a second because Krash had answered the phone. "Dude be in Scutterfield, baby," she said, trying not to say too much.

"How did you find out so fast?" Krash asked, surprised. He listened intently as Trina told him what Midnight had told her about Dirty having to leave town.

"When I asked if Twin went with him, she told me that he never leaves Scutterfield because he be chasing that money," Trina continued.

"Are you still going to pick Midnight up?" Krash asked.

"We about to leave the house now," Trina replied.

"Well, Keebler said to take his car because I'm following him in mines," Krash said.

Trina told Zya what he said, then ended the call so they could get ready to ride out.

"So, are you going to tell me what our men do?" Zya asked again as they hopped in the Crown Vic.

"You really don't know, do you?" Trina asked from the passenger seat as she lit a blunt.

Zya glanced over at her just as she was pulling off but had to refocus on the road because of the powerful motor threatening to get away from her. Once she got control of the car, she looked back over at Trina, waiting on an answer.

"I thought they were dopeboys at first, but I don't think so now," Zya said once she figured out Trina wouldn't say much.

"The easiest way for me to say this would be to say they are hustlers in the game," Trina said as she passed the blunt. "They do a little bit of everything," she continued.

"I was just asking because I have a cousin who just died, and I wanted Keebler to meet him, but when I said his name, I saw a look in his eyes that scared me," Zya explained.

"For real? What was his name," Trina asked.

"Godzilla," Zya replied like Trina wouldn't know who he was, but she got a different reply. "You knew Godzilla?" Zya asked.

Regaining her composure like Krash had taught her to do, Trina smiled. "Who don't know Godzilla? He's been known for killing niggas for years," she said. She hoped Zya would leave the subject alone because there would be no easy way to tell her that her man was responsible for the death of her cousin. There was something that she needed to know, though.

"How is it your cousin is Godzilla, but you've never heard of Keebler and Krash?" Trina asked.

"Unless they fucked with cuz, I couldn't tell you shit about a lot of niggas out here," Zya admitted honestly.

Trina looked over at her friend and saw the squareness about her. "Have you heard any of the rumors about Godzilla?" Trina asked.

"Yes, and those same rumors have run off a few men in my life," Zya admitted.

"Well, multiply those stories time four, and you have our men," Trina said seriously.

"What?!" Zya asked. "My baby may be a lot of things, but he ain't that ruthless," she continued in disbelief.

"Oh. Okay. I'll let Midnight back up everything I'm saying, and I won't have to say a word. Just ask her," Trina said.

"You ask her for me," Zya said back.

They had been so deep in conversation that they were now pulling up at Midnight's house without realizing it. As soon as they were safely in the driveway, Zya blew the horn. Less than a minute later, Midnight came outside, smiling as she hopped in the car.

"Let me find out you hoes trying to start Crown Vic club," Midnight said jokingly as she relaxed in the backseat of the car. Before she got cool with Trina and Zya, she had never actually ridden in either Crown Vic, and she had to admit that she liked how both vehicles rode.

"Ain't no sense in letting the boys have all the fun," Zya replied to the comment.

"If my dumb-ass nigga keep pulling the shit he's pulling, I may have to upgrade to a man with a Crown Vic," Midnight said.

"You just looking for a reason to fuck with that boy again," Zya spoke.

"Ain't nothing wrong with finding a good nigga to be down with," Trina said. "You just better understand that if Dirty's bad ass find out, he gone crash out on both of y'all," she continued.

"Well, he need to get his shit in order. How he gone dip out of town without telling me?" Midnight asked, getting mad all over again.

"Maybe he had some business to handle, and he didn't wanna risk you getting hurt," Zya said, trying to sound reasonable, but the only thing she got was uncontrollable laughter from both women.

"We a team, bitch. I ain't new to shit," Midnight said without saying too much, but she would have to say more because Zya didn't understand.

"Let her know what's up with you, and at the same time, tell her what kind of dude she has compared to her cousin Godzilla," Trina said while looking Midnight in the eyes to let her know to watch what she said.

"She's not familiar with the lifestyle?" Midnight asked while smiling.

"What lifestyle?" Zya asked.

"This lifestyle," Midnight said and pulled out a black Glock .40 from her purse. Zya saw the pistol through the rearview mirror and nodded.

She was used to being around guns, so that was nothing surprising. The stories that came behind it, though, brought a lot of questions to surface. Luckily for her, Trina and Midnight answered all the questions as honestly as they could. By the time they finally made it back to Coro Lake, Zya had received a history lesson that made her love Keebler even more.

15

After Krash hung up with Trina, he immediately called Keebler. "What's the word?" Keebler answered.

"It looks like Dirty decided to dip for a while so he wouldn't have to choose sides when the shit hit the fan," Krash said.

"What?" Keebler asked in disbelief.

"Baby said Midnight is mad because bruh left her a letter saying he had to go out of town to handle some business," Krash explained. Keebler just laughed because he knew the letter was bullshit. "She also told me where Twin at," Krash continued.

"Where?" Keebler asked, all business once again.

"Scutterfield," Krash replied. "The way I see it is we can ride through Tank's old hood and start some shit. Then we ride through Scutterfield before word gets out and close shit down," he continued.

"Say no more," Keebler said, then ended the call.

Krash found a spot to park his car that he was cool with and that was close to the interstate ramp on Danny Thomas. As soon as he was in the SS Impala, Keebler sped off. Since the plan was already laid out, as soon as they pulled up on the block, Keebler stopped in the middle of the street and put the car in Park. Without warning, they both hopped out with a rifle in their hands.

Doom! Doom! Doom! Doom! Doom! Doom! Doom! Doom!

The rifles were so loud that it sounded like thunder was erupting through the skies. But that was just part of the terror. Each round fired was doing damage everywhere it went, and people ran for cover, trying not to get gunned down.

Keebler was first to stop shooting so he could jump back behind the wheel and put the car in gear. When Krash finally hopped in, they sped away from the scene without giving themselves a chance to check out their work.

"One more stop. Then we burn this bitch down," Keebler said, speaking on the car. Krash just smiled as he reloaded both rifles for round two.

Twin and Ya-Yo were on the block with some other hustlers getting money when the SS Impala swerved on the block. Twin immediately got on point in case it was the undercovers trying to bust them, but Ya-Yo acted as if he wasn't worried. Before they had the chance to react, Keebler and Krash hopped out with rifles in hand and continued their reign of terror.

Doom! Doom! Doom! Doom! Doom! Doom! Doom! Doom!

They fired rounds on everybody outside, hitting most of their targets. Twin managed to get away with some of the other hustlers, but he would find out later that Ya-Yo hadn't been so lucky.

Once Keebler and Krash felt like they'd made their point, they sped off just as quick as they'd pulled up on the block. Without a word, they headed to the Crown Vic.

"Do your thang," Krash told Keebler once they were at the car. He quickly loaded the rifles in the backseat of his car while Keebler set the SS Impala on fire.

"Let's head to the crib," Keebler hopped in the passenger seat and said with a smile. Krash sped off before the other car went up in heavy flames.

"You think we got our point across?" Krash asked suddenly.

"That was just to let the young nigga know he done crossed the line," Keebler replied. "Twin gotta die, and that's that," he continued. Krash already knew that once Keebler set his mind on something, there was no sense arguing with him, and this time was no different. Whether Twin knew it or not, his days were now numbered.

***

On the outskirts of the city, a meeting was taking place, and Keebler was the topic of conversation. Dirty had actually left the state, but it wasn't for the reasons people suspected. He'd received a text that he just couldn't ignore, instructing him to meet up immediately.

Now, as he pulled up at the Harrah's Resort Hotel in Tunica, Mississippi, Dirty prayed he wouldn't be forced to do something he didn't want to do. After finding a parking spot, he was met at the entrance by two men who not only looked dangerous, but the bulges under their shirts let it be known that they meant business. They got on the elevator and went up to the eighth floor without saying one word. As soon as they entered the suite, the two men got physical, stripping Dirty of his pistol.

"Have a seat, Dirty," a familiar voice spoke suddenly.

"Was that necessary?" Dirty asked as he headed toward the voice.

"With everything that's happened, I can't trust anyone right now," the man spoke.

"You can always trust me, Smoove," Dirty answered.

"We're about to find out," Smoove stated firmly. "Who is this?" he asked before showing him the picture that had been found in Godzilla's phone. It was the same picture sent to him, so Dirty knew then how serious the meeting was.

"That's Keebler," Dirty said like the picture meant nothing.

"You know that we know Godzilla depended on you whenever he wanted a job done," Smoove said slowly. Dirty just nodded as an answer. "I know he sent this picture to you. That's why I asked you to come see me. What I wanna know is why Godzilla had beef with this man. And does he have anything to do with his death?" Smoove asked.

"All I know is he wanted to know where Keebler laid his head. I don't know what the beef was about," Dirty said, telling half the truth.

"Did you find out anything?" Smoove asked.

"Everything happened so fast, I didn't bother to keep looking after the shooting," Dirty admitted.

"How much would it cost to put you on my payroll?" Smoove asked. He wanted to have a talk with Keebler before he decided whether to kill the man.

"It depends on what you need me for," Dirty said. "I usually eliminate people when Godzilla calls me, but I can see you don't need my help in that area," he continued while nodding at the four men posted around the suite.

Smoove smiled at the young hitman. "I need to speak with Keebler. Can you find him for me?" he asked. "Before you reply, please understand that if you take my money and don't deliver in a timely manner, the same price will be on your head," he continued as plainly as he could.

For a second, Dirty just stared at the man, trying to figure out if he was being threatened. He had to smile to keep from wigging out and losing his life. "I know you're head of the Black Gorilla Cartel and all, but I don't do good under pressure, and I don't take threats lightly," Dirty stated.

"There is no pressure because you don't have to take the job. And I don't make threats, Dirty. If I say you die, then you'll die," Smoove said with finality.

"Let me think on it for a while. I'll give you my answer in 24 hours," Dirty assured the man. He was starting to get a bad vibe from the man, so he was ready to go.

"I'll contact you in 24 hours," Smoove said with a head nod.

Two of the four men then escorted Dirty out of the suite and down to the parking lot where they gave him the gun back. Dirty hopped in his BMW and headed back to the city limits to find Keebler and Krash to warn them.

***

Back in Scutterfield, Twin eased back up to the block in search of Ya-Yo. They lost contact with each other during the shooting, and now he was thinking the worst.

"Have you seen my brother?" he asked another hustler who was standing around watching the police try to piece together what had just happened.

"I think that's his body over there," dude said while pointing at a body under a white sheet by one of the neighboring yards' fences. Twin tried to walk over to the body but was stopped a police officer.

"You can't go over there, son," the officer said.

"I need to see if that's my brother," Twin said, sounding like a kid. He gave the officer the description of Ya-Yo, then watched as the man went over to the body. He caught a glimpse of the shoes and knew right then it was Ya-Yo even before the officer confirmed it.

As he walked away, Twin tried to come to grips with everything that was going on. Was the recent shooting retaliation for him shooting Big Dee, or did it have anything to do with Tank? There was only one way for him to find out. He pulled out his phone and made a call.

***

When Krash pulled up at the house, the smell of barbecue made the men's stomachs growl.

"I guess it's true that working hard makes you hungry," Keebler said while rubbing his stomach.

Krash just laughed because for once, one of Keebler's corny remarks was true. "Let's go get something to eat," he said, then led the way to the house while hiding the rifles under his arms.

When they stepped inside, the smell of weed was so loud, it was a wonder they couldn't smell it outside. Keebler followed Krash to put the rifles up, and it surprised Keebler that Krash had decided not to throw them away. The expression on his face must've shocked Krash because he felt the need to explain himself.

"Since we started the war against Twin with the .223s, I figured we may as well keep them until the job is complete," he said.

"Say no more. Let's go get some food and a blunt to smoke," Keebler replied as they headed to the kitchen.

They found the girls outside by the lake smoking blunts while Trina kept an eye on the grill.

"Hey, baby," Krash said in his deep voice as he gave Trina a hug from the back. All she could do was purr like a kitten, which made Zya and Midnight turn around to see what was going on.

"Hey, boo," Zya jumped up saying as she ran into her man's arms. The two couples kissed each other, and then the men turned their attention to Midnight.

"What it do?" Keebler asked, smiling. It was really the first time they'd ever kicked it with Midnight without Dirty being around.

"What y'all been up to?" Midnight asked as she gave both men a hug. They were her brothers, and she knew they would keep her safe.

"Just taking care of business as usual," Keebler said with a smile. She smiled back, letting him know she understood.

"Where your boy at?" he asked suddenly, making the smile vanish.

"He dipped off without me," Midnight said through gritted teeth. She then explained how he'd left a letter on the nightstand for her to find instead of waking her up to see if she wanted to tag along.

***

Dirty was halfway back to the city limits when he got a call from his cousin. He was hesitant to answer since he knew what he'd done, but he wanted to hear his side of it.

"Yeah," he answered on the fourth ring.

"What's good?" Twin asked, trying to break the ice.

"Shit, you tell me," Dirty replied. "Why did you ride through the south like that without finishing the job?" he asked.

"Dude sold me a brick that came from one of my brothers," Twin said. When Dirty didn't reply, he knew he needed to explain more. "That same brother was robbed and killed the other day," he continued.

Dirty understood the situation a little more, even though it still didn't explain everything.

"Cuz, dude didn't die, and there's some people about to come holler at you. Some real bad people," Dirty explained.

"Somebody just rode through the hood and shot it up," Twin told him. "I don't know if it's retaliation for that or because of what happened to my brother," he continued. He needed to know how to come back from everything and who to bring the noise to.

"I just got back to the city. Let me ride around and see if I can find out anything. Until I get back to you, stay out the streets," Dirty expressed firmly, then ended the call.

After Dirty left the resort, Smoove had two of his men follow him to see if he would lead them to Keebler. Since he hadn't decided if he would help them, Smoove gave specific orders that if Dirty was seen talking to Keebler before deciding to work with them, they were to take the young hitman out. Now, the black Lincoln followed the black Beamer into the city from a distance.

***

Back in Coro Lake, Midnight was enjoying herself until her phone started ringing.

"Hello," she answered on the second ring like she didn't have an attitude.

"Where you at, baby?" Dirty's voice came through.

"Over Trina's house," Midnight told him. She may have been mad at him, but he was still her man.

"How you get over there?" Dirty asked.

"I had them come get me since you just decided to go out of town without at least checking to see if I wanted to go," Midnight said, letting her true feelings come out.

"Baby, listen," Dirty said and then explained where he'd gone, why he went there, and who he went to meet. "Is either big bruh around?" he asked.

"They're both here. Hold on," Midnight said and gave Keebler the phone.

"What's the business?" Keebler hopped on the phone and asked.

"We need to meet asap," Dirty said.

"Come to the crib," Keebler suggested, but Dirty refused.

"I don't know if I'm being followed, so it's best we meet on neutral grounds and in a public place," he explained.

"Where you wanna meet?" Keebler asked.

"Wherever you feel comfortable," Dirty said.

"Meet us at the South Third Shopping Center in twenty minutes," Keebler instructed.

"Bet," Dirty quickly agreed and ended the call.

Midnight took the phone back and put it to her ear. "He could've at least said bye," she said before throwing the phone in her purse.

"Look, we gotta go meet lil bruh. Midnight, I want you to stay here until we get back," Keebler explained, then nodded to Krash that it was time to roll out.

16

Twin didn't know how to take what his cousin had just told him, and he still didn't know what actions caused the drive-by that killed Ya-Yo. There was one thing that he did know, and that was the surviving victim had to go if he didn't want to end up with a case. After he had been shot four times in the chest, there was no doubt that he was still in the hospital. The question was: how would he be able to get close enough to finish what he started? Disregarding what his cousin had just said, Twin jumped in his Cutlass and sped off.

***

After everything Keebler had just told his best friend, Krash decided to take Trina's red Toyota Camry since it was low-key and under tinted windows.

"I don't think I ever rode in something this small," Keebler said as he got comfortable in the passenger seat.

"Don't be fooled by the Toyota logo. This bitch can get down with the best of them," Krash said, then sped off to show how much power was under the hood.

"It's nice for a female," Keebler said as he lit the blunt Zya gave him as they were leaving.

"What you think about what Dirty said?" Krash asked suddenly.

"I don't know how to take that shit," Keebler replied while passing him the blunt. "If he had some foul shit on his mind, he could've just brought it to the crib. I offered to tell him where we were," he continued.

"He could've thought against it since Midnight is there," Krash said through coughs. The comment had Keebler thinking. "Just be on point when we get there," Krash continued after a brief silence.

***

Just as Dirty pulled up at the shopping center, he got another call from Twin.

"What's up?" he answered on the second ring.

"Where you at, cuz?" Twin asked.

"About to meet up with my guys to see if I can end this bullshit," Dirty admitted.

"If they had anything to do with Tank dying, ain't no ending it," Twin admitted.

Dirty instantly came up with an idea. Maybe if he put both parties in front of each other, they'd talk everything out instead of continuing the pistol playing.

"Meet me at the shopping center on Third Street," Dirty suggested.

"I'll be there in a few," Twin told him and ended the call. Somebody had to pay for Ya-Yo's death, and he may as well start showing everybody what the consequences would be for disrespecting what he loved.

Dirty found a parking spot where they'd have some privacy and at the same time could see every entrance to the lot in case someone wanted to ambush them.

Not even five minutes later, the Toyota Camry cautiously pulled up on the lot. Krash checked the surroundings for anything out of the ordinary while Keebler searched for the black BMW.

"There he go right there," he said while pointing.

Across the lot, Dirty sat patiently under the tinted windows.

"You think he'll be surprised when we pull up next to him?" Krash asked as they cruised to where he was parked.

"I don't know, but I bet he watching us right now," Keebler replied. Because of everything that was going on, Krash decided not to spook the man, so he rolled down his window just as he pulled up next to the driver's side window. "Bet you didn't expect us to pull up in no shit like this," Keebler yelled out the window with a smile.

"As clean as this junt is, I know it can't be hot," Dirty said as he checked out the 18-inch rims.

"This is Trina's whip. We felt the need to switch it up a bit after your last conversation," Krash said.

"Respect," Dirty said smiling.

"So, what's going on?" Keebler asked suddenly.

Across the lot in the black Lincoln, Smoove's men were trying to get a good look at the driver of the Camry. They knew there were two people in the vehicle, but because of the way they were parked and the tinted windows, they could only see the driver. The man in the passenger seat called Smoove to let him know what was going on. After hearing that he wanted them to continue following Dirty, they sat back and waited to see what the young hitman's next move would be. Then, all of a sudden, everything got crazy real quick.

Dirty spotted the Cutlass pulling up just as he was explaining his meeting with Smoove. He was about to let them know his cousin was pulling up on the other side of the Camry but paused mid-sentence when he saw the pistol come out the driver's side window.

Boc! Boc! Boc! Boc! Boc! Boc!

Twin let off round after round into the Camry and continued shooting until Krash sped off.

"I'm hit!" Keebler yelled as Krash sped out into traffic in the shot-up car. "Who was that?" he asked.

"You wouldn't believe me if I told you," Krash said as he sped up Third Street.

Unsure how bad his best friend had been hit, he headed toward Regional One Hospital since it was the closest to their location. When he looked over at Keebler and saw his bloody shirt, it only made him push the car harder.

"Just hold on, nigga! Don't you die on me before we finish what we started," Krash said.

Keebler was in so much pain, he couldn't speak. All he did was moan out loud, but he prayed to make it through so he could terrorize whoever was behind the shooting.

***

"Did you see that shit?" the driver of the Lincoln asked the passenger.

"That looked like something straight from the movies," the passenger replied.

What was even more shocking to them was the fact that Dirty was still parked like nothing had happened. He just sat there looking at the shooter and shaking his head.

"He knows the shooter," the passenger said, then called Smoove back to tell him what had just happened. It wasn't until sirens could be heard that Dirty finally decided to pull off.

"He's on the move," the driver said as he pulled off to follow him. They pulled out the shopping center going one way, while Twin sped off in the other direction.

Dirty sped up Third Street going the same way he saw Krash speed off in, while dialing numbers on his phone.

"What, cuz?" Twin answered like he had an attitude.

"What the fuck were you thinking?" Dirty asked hysterically.

"I told you what was up," Twin stated. "Them niggas killed my big bruh. Now, they gotta pay," he continued.

"Do you know why I asked you to meet me at the shopping center?" Dirty asked. He then explained how he wanted both groups to talk face to face so they could get to the bottom of the accusations. "Now, you got it looking like I set them up, and the last thing I need is enemies like them," Dirty explained.

"You're a killer, cuz. Just take them out like you do everybody else," Twin said, still not fully understanding how serious the situation was.

"Who do you think gave me the game?" Dirty asked. The quietness over the phone let him know that he finally had his cousin's attention. "Get off the streets and stay off until you hear from me," he told Twin.

"You're not worried about them niggas thinking you set them up?" Twin asked.

"The only way to show them I didn't is to step to them and explain myself. Hopefully, they'll believe me. If I do die, get outta town fast, kinfolk," Dirty said and ended the call. He didn't know where Krash had gone, but if they'd been hit, he figured they would head to a hospital. He decided to ride downtown while he tried to contact them.

***

Krash pulled up in front of Regional One Hospital like he didn't have a care in the world. Two police standing outside were about to tell him to move the car until they saw it was riddled with bullets on the passenger side. Instead, they went over and helped get Keebler out the car while he screamed in pain as they carried him into the hospital. Once the doctors took over, those same officers tried to question Krash, but he gave them the cold shoulder. Their number one rule was to never talk to the police about anything, and he didn't intend to break the code.

As he went back outside to inspect the damage to the car, he could hear his phone ringing. When he looked at the number, Krash almost ignored the call, but he decided to give them the benefit of the doubt. "Hello," he answered in a tone that was deeper than usual.

"Big bruh! I didn't have nothing to do with that," Dirty immediately said. "My kinfolk has lost his mind. He seems to think y'all robbed and killed his homeboys. That's why he shot Big Dee," he explained.

"All that sounds good, but how did he know we would be at the shopping center?" Krash asked. As mad as he was about the situation, it was hard for him to accept that Dirty may have crossed them, so he would give him the benefit of the doubt.

"I wanted y'all to get together and talk this shit out. I had no clue cuz would pull up busting," Dirty said.

Krash thought about it, and it did make sense, but the final decision on how this would play out with him was on Keebler since he was the one who got shot.

"Where you at now?" Krash asked.

"Heading downtown. I figured if one y'all was shot, you'd go to the hospital," Dirty replied. He could hear a small chuckle through the phone and knew he must've been right.

"Look, Keebler was hit, and he's being tended to by the doctors right now. Head to Regional One, and you can explain yourself to him," Krash said. "But if I see your cousin anywhere near here, I will kill him," he continued.

"You don't have to worry about that, big bruh. I'll be pulling up in a few," Dirty said and ended the call. He shook his head at the thought of Keebler being hit because he knew Twin would have to pay.

***

Back in South Memphis, Flea was on the grind as usual, even though his mind was on Big Dee. He stayed at the hospital with Twoine until the early morning. Now he was surprised when he got a call from Twoine saying Krash and Keebler were at the hospital. He thought they'd gone up there to check on Big Dee until Twoine let him know the real reason for the visit.

"One of your boys got shot," Twoine told him.

"I'm on the way up there now," Flea replied, already walking toward his Crown Vic. So much was going on in the streets that he was now thinking of buying a pistol for protection. His next move depended on what he saw once he got to the hospital.

***

While Krash waited for Dirty to pull up, he continued checking out the Camry, and to his surprise, it wasn't as bad as he first figured. He would have the passenger seat replaced because of the blood and have the bullet holes in the passenger side doors plugged before repainting the entire car.

Dirty came speeding around the corner and parked behind the Camry. "How bad is it?" Dirty hopped out the Beamer and asked.

"He's still in there with the doctors, but it looked bad when we got here," Krash said while watching his reaction.

"I don't know what cuz is thinking about," Dirty said while shaking his head. It felt like he was being torn between two groups of family members. While Twin was actually a family member, Krash and Keebler had been there for him when he was at rock bottom.

"Did y'all have something to do with his homeboy dying?" he asked.

"Dude was just another victim to the shit as far as I'm concerned," Krash said honestly. "That didn't have nothing to do with your cousin, though," he continued.

The two men just stared at each other until Flea came speeding up the street with his system blasting.

"I'm ridin' around town with the top blown off/

Four niggas deep, ridin' with a sawed off/

Lookin' for some hoes that's a bit throwed off/

It ain't tricking if you got it, mane, so I'm a show off"

Flea sat there rapping his music while Krash and Dirty nodded their heads to the beat. He let a verse play before he finally hopped out.

"Who shit is that, and where can I get it?" Dirty asked as Flea gave them dap.

"That's my shit. It'll be on my mixtape," Flea said proudly.

"You been holding back on us, I see," Krash spoke up.

"You know I can't give out all my music. Gotta keep the fans wanting more," Flea preached.

"I can dig it," Krash said, laughing.

Flea turned his attention to the shot-up Toyota Camry and began looking inside at the blood-stained seat. "I take it the message I got about Keebler is true?" he asked Krash.

"What was the message?" Krash asked hesitantly. As far as he knew, nobody knew they were at the hospital.

"Twoine hit me up and said Keebler had been shot," Flea said.

"It's true," Dirty half-whispered.

"What happened? And do I need to strap up?" Flea asked.

"Before we get into that, let's go check up on my nigga," Krash suggested, then led the way back in the hospital.

The trio was led to a room where they found Keebler laid back on a bed with his left side bandaged up.

"I see you still pushing like a G," Krash walked in saying. He tried to give him dap, but Keebler was looking at Dirty like he was waiting for an explanation.

"I didn't have nothing to do with it, bruh. All I wanted to do was end the suspicions before it got to the pistols," Dirty explained.

"But you knew that nigga was coming to the meeting spot, and you didn't forewarn us?" Keebler asked in a brotherly tone.

"Yes," Dirty answered like a child.

Flea just watched in amazement at the way they really acted like they were family. If he really knew how far back the relationship went, he would've understood. "What's going on?" Flea asked.

"Tell him," Krash said.

"My cousin shot Big Dee and Keebler," Dirty admitted.

"There's only one way for you to make this right," Keebler spoke up again.

Dirty just nodded because he knew what he had to do to save his life. Flea didn't know what they were talking about, but his mind was made up about getting a pistol. Too many people close to him were getting hit for him to risk getting caught slipping.

"So what did the doctors say about your condition?" Flea suddenly asked. "It looks a lot worse than it really is. They wanted to keep me here for a couple of days, but I ain't trying to hear that. I got a fine nurse at the crib waiting on me," Keebler said.

"Shit, we gone get cursed the fuck out first," Krash told them.

"How long before they let you go?" Flea asked.

"I'm waiting for them to bring me the discharge papers now," Keebler said. "It may be an hour or two, though," he continued.

"Well, I'm about to go check on Big Dee. Text me if y'all get ready to leave before I get back," Flea told him.

"Hold on. I'll go with you," Dirty said. Krash promised to let them know if they were leaving, then watched as they walked out the room.

"What do you think?" Keebler asked once they were alone in the room. Krash didn't have to ask what he was talking about because he was just about to ask the same question.

"I think he's telling the truth," Krash said after really thinking about the situation. "I feel we at least owe him the benefit of the doubt. Let's see if and how long it takes him to bring his cousin to us," he continued.

"What if he decides not to?" Keebler asked just as a doctor walked in. They ended the conversation for the time being as Keebler got his bandages replaced and was then told he was ready to go. The doctor left, leaving them alone again.

"If he refuse to bring us Twin, then we gotta do what we gotta do," Krash spoke. Keebler just nodded as he led the way out the hospital room.

They could hear laughing coming from Big Dee's room, so they decided to crash the party.

"You youngsters know that a party ain't a party without some OGs in the mix," Keebler said as they entered the room.

"They releasing you already?" Big Dee asked, disappointed.

"My wounds are superficial," Keebler told him. "How much longer they talking about keeping you?" he asked.

"I don't know, but my grandma is stressing about not being able to pay the hospital bill," Big Dee told them.

"Don't worry about the bill, young nigga. Just get well so you can get about your hustle 'cause we got plenty of bricks to get off," Keebler said.

Twoine had been quiet since they came to the room, but now he was all ears. "What about me? Y'all still going to look out for me?" he asked.

"Finish what we asked you to do, and I personally got you," Krash answered. Flea looked over at his homeboy and nodded.

"I don't mean to be a party pooper, but I'm ready to get home to my girl," Keebler said. "Flea, you feel like giving us a ride?" he asked.

"You know I got you, but what about the Camry?" Flea asked.

"I called a tow truck to take it to the shop already. It should be gone," Krash explained.

"What about me?" Dirty asked.

"You have some business to take care of before we have that trust in you again," Keebler stated firmly. With that said, everybody said their goodbyes and left Twoine to keep an eye on Big Dee.

***

The men in the black Lincoln were parked outside the hospital in a parking lot where they could keep an eye on the black BMW. They had been patiently waiting for Dirty to come out the hospital, even after seeing the Camry being towed away. Smoove had called to check on them, and after hearing nothing new had turned up, he was about to end the call until the passenger stopped him. They were looking at Dirty and three other men get in the cars.

"You ain't gone believe this, boss," the passenger said as he began taking pictures for proof of what he was looking at.

17

After Smoove saw the pictures of Dirty with Keebler then heard about how they met up as soon as he left Tunica, Smoove felt like a fool.

"Load the boys up and let's ride out," he told the other two bodyguards. They left the room and headed to the parking lot, where they found two tinted vans parked by the other black Lincoln Smoove was in. They loaded up the vehicles and headed to Memphis.

Dirty was real disappointed that Keebler didn't want to know where they were staying, especially since he'd been invited only hours ago. Now, he was forced to choose to either ride with Twin and possibly be put on the hitlist himself or ride for the only people who showed him love when he didn't have a pot to piss in. He weighed his options as he headed to the north side to have a word with Twin.

When he pulled up in Scutterfield, the first thing he noticed was the crime scene tape blocking off the street where the traphouse was.

"I forgot cuz said said somebody shot the block up," he told himself as he turned around. He pulled over to the curb and thought about the situation at hand. "I know what I need to do," Dirty said after being in deep thought for a few minutes. He called Twin as he pulled back into traffic.

"What's good?" Twin answered like he didn't have a care in the world. The fact that Dirty was calling back meant he talked his way out of being a target, and he couldn't live with his family dying because of something he did.

"I just went to Scutterfield looking for you. Y'all done pissed somebody off bad," Dirty said, laughing.

"I told you," Twin reminded him. "We need to meet up and discuss how to handle this situation you're in," Dirty stated firmly.

"You'll have to come to me because I'm on my way to get something to eat," Twin told him.

"Where you going?" Dirty asked.

"Logan's Roadhouse in Southaven," Twin told him.

"Why you riding all the way to Mississippi for something to eat?" Dirty asked, confused.

"It's too hot to be in the city right now, and a nigga gotta be crazy to come through Mississippi on that bullshit. These white folks hiding a nigga," Twin said and laughed. His cousin laughed with him because it was true.

"I'm on my way now," Dirty said and ended the call.

***

The girls had finally finished barbecuing and had moved the party indoors when they heard a loud system pulling up in front of the house. Trina immediately became suspicious because her car didn't have a loud system in it, so she went to the front door to see who it was with the girls on her tail.

"Hello," Midnight said out loud when she saw the silver Crown Vic pulling up in the driveway.

"Control yourself, girl," Zya said while smiling. Trina was trying to figure out why he was at the house until three of the doors opened and she saw her man hop out. When she saw Keebler bandaged up, the first thing that came to mind was that they were in an accident.

"What happened to you?" Zya asked as soon as the men all walked in the house.

"I got shot," Keebler said as he found a seat.

"Where's my car?" Zya asked.

"It's in the shop," Krash admitted, then explained what happened.

Flea and Midnight tried to act like nothing was going on between them in front of Keebler and Krash, but they weren't fooling anybody.

"Where's Dirty right now?" Midnight asked after hearing about the shooting.

"Trying to right a wrong, I hope," Keebler replied. "He won't be popping up at the house if that's what you and Flea are worried about," he continued with a smile.

"What you talking about?" Flea asked like he didn't have a clue about what was being said.

"Y'all aint fooling nobody. I saw it in your eyes when we were at the hospital for Big Dee," Keebler explained. "I ain't mad at you, Midnight. My nigga got it going on," he continued.

"Who you telling?" Midnight said.

"Just don't let Dirty find out," Keebler warned.

"Y'all wanna go to the studio?" Flea asked suddenly. The sun had finally gone down all the way, and he was in the mood to make some music. Everybody agreed that getting out the house sounded good, so after the men made plates to go, they all headed to the east side in all three Crown Vics.

***

Dirty had to admit that he enjoyed himself with his cousin, which only made what he would end up doing more painful. They had a good steak dinner before Dirty wanted to go check up on his new friend, so he said his goodbyes and headed back to Memphis.

His first stop was in South Memphis, where he knew Flea spent most of his days hustling. The other hustlers were now used to seeing the black Beamer on the block, so instead of dipping off, they just kept an eye on the vehicle. He didn't see the Crown Vic at the traphouse, so he just kept driving.

"It's dark, so he probably at the studio," Dirty told himself as he headed to the east side, hoping he could remember where the house was.

Kojak had a session already rolling as usual, but he was glad to see Flea because it always meant more money.

"I hope we didn't catch you at a bad time," Flea said as he led the way into the house.

"If I say you're welcome anytime, that's what I mean," Kojak said while giving him dap. He spoke to everyone else as he locked the front door back, then led the way to the studio. There were way more people in the room than there were last time, but the vibe was good and Kojak knew the two groups would get along.

"Well, just chill out and make yourselves at home," Kojak told them, then went back to working with the dude sitting in the booth. He hit a button on his equipment, and a beat that immediately got Flea's attention came on. He pulled out a sack of weed and gave it to Midnight before walking over to where Kojak was. He didn't say anything at first, but when the chorus popped in, he knew he had to get on that track.

"Who is that in the booth?" Flea asked.

"That's Mac Poo-Poo. He's a South Memphis nigga himself," Kojak said.

"I can hear it in his lyrics. That's probably why I'm feeling his music," Flea said. "And why I gotta be on this song," he continued as Kojak laughed.

"That might be what it's missing too," Kojak admitted as he thought about it.

He let Mac Poo-Poo go over the track again before going to see what he thought about adding Flea to the track. He wasn't shocked to find out Mac Poo-Poo was familiar with Flea since he was a real hustler, but it wasn't for that reason. Mac Poo-Poo had heard some of Flea's music, so working with him on the music tip was something he'd already thought of.

Flea decided to make him an offer. "Tell Mac Poo-Poo if he let me get on this joint here, he can lay down a verse on some of my trap music," he told Kojak.

"Get ready to go in the booth," Kojak told him because he already knew what the answer would be.

***

Dirty was surprised he found the studio, but he was even more shocked to find Krash and Keebler's cars parked behind Flea's. After the earlier events, Dirty knew for sure that their girls wouldn't let them out of their sights, and Midnight was with the girls, so he wondered if she was at the studio. He knew better than to just pop up since he was not invited. That would make it look like he was following them when he was supposed to be delivering Twin's head to them on a silver platter.

Instead, he decided to call and ask Midnight where she was. The voicemail picked up on the second ring, which meant she intentionally ignored the call, and he was starting to feel some type of way. He pulled up the street and parked where he could see the front door without his car being seen. For some reason, every time Dirty thought about Midnight, he got a bad vibe. He was debating whether to crash the party when he spotted a black Lincoln followed by two tinted out vans creep down the block with the lights off. Thinking it was the police, he backed up the street until he got a safe distance away before turning the lights on and speeding off.

***

It took Flea and Mac Poo-Poo no time to collaborate. Now Kojak was putting his stank on it while they sat back smoking blunts.

"What part of South Memphis you be at?" Mac Poo-Poo asked.

"I'm from Glenview," Flea said proudly. "Mostly on the other side of the tracks by Rozelle Elementary," he continued.

"We from the Willett Projects," Mac Poo-Poo said. They just laughed because they were from the same area. Only some train tracks separated the two hoods. Now that they'd hooked up in the booth, Flea gave Mac Poo-Poo his number so they could stay in contact.

***

Outside the studio, Smoove was parked on the next street while the hit team went to handle business. Minutes had passed, and there was still no gunfire, so Smoove had his driver pull off to see what was happening. They were met by the two men in the other Lincoln and the two vans.

"He's vanished, boss," the driver told him immediately.

"How did it happen?" Smoove asked calmly.

"We saw where he'd parked at, but when we pulled up, he was gone," the driver explained. Smoove was thinking that maybe Dirty had spotted them tailing him and managed to give them the slip.

"How long do you think it'll take to find him?" Smoove asked.

"We know several areas he was in. If he frequents any one of them, we'll be back on his tail in a day or two," the passenger spoke up.

"Make it happen," Smoove said. He was about to have his driver pull off until he was stopped.

"Boss, that car was parked behind his at the hospital. They were together until they left going their separate ways. It's possible he was going to this house," the passenger explained.

Smoove checked out all the custom vehicles parked at the house and weighed his options. Besides the three Crown Victorias parked at the curb, there was a black Expedition sitting on some big rims and a candy apple red Cadillac parked in the driveway. He decided not to do anything that would risk getting innocent people hurt.

"Just focus on Dirty right now. Find him and keep him in your sight," Smoove said and tapped his driver to pull off.

***

"Shit, we about to roll out," Mac Poo-Poo told Flea after he got a copy of the music they dropped.

"That's what's up. Make sure you hit me up when you wanna come back for another session," Flea reminded the man. He then gave Mac Poo-Poo an ounce of weed for him and his brothers to smoke. "That's the mildest shit I sell. I got some real blueberry Kush if you want it as well," he continued.

"'Preciate it, bruh," Mac Poo-Poo said as he gave Flea dap. He then nodded at Krash and Keebler before following Kojak to the front door.

Just as Mac Poo-Poo stepped to his Expedition, he caught a glimpse at the second van as it sped up the street. He instantly got a bad vibe, but it wasn't because he thought it was the police like Dirty did. Something told him that it was a hit team on the prowl, and he did not want to get caught up, so he told his brothers to get in the Expedition. When he pulled off, he went the same direction Dirty did to make sure they didn't cross paths with the van.

Not long after Mac Poo-Poo left, Flea was making copies of his latest music for them to ride home to.

"Are you chilling with me tonight?" Flea asked Midnight.

"Yes," Midnight replied after thinking about it. Since she didn't have to hide it from Krash and Keebler anymore, they would be able to spend more time together.

Flea paid Kojak for the night's session and then passed out the rest of the weed he had on him before finally preparing to leave.

"Let me holler at you right quick," Keebler told Flea once they were at the cars. Flea unlocked the car and started it up so Midnight could get comfortable before going to see what the man wanted.

"What's up, big bruh?" Flea asked with a smile.

"Watch yourself with Midnight, homie. If Dirty finds out about you two, he will come at you full speed, and we won't be able to stop him," Keebler stated firmly.

"I know, bruh, and I got this," Flea said reassuringly. "We have a real connection that's too strong for us to stop. I want to be with her, but she's hesitant about leaving Dirty," he continued.

"Maybe because she know what the consequences will be," Krash said as he walked up.

"I feel y'all, and I promise to be careful," Flea told them.

"Alright," both men said and left it alone. They all got in their cars with their girls and sped off.

While Keebler followed Krash back to the Coro Lake, Flea and Midnight headed to the Peabody Hotel downtown.

"You know you don't have to spend all this money for a night at this expensive hotel," Midnight told Flea as they parked.

"You deserve the best at all times," Flea replied as he stared into her eyes.

"If you knew the real me, you wouldn't feel that way," Midnight told him.

"I couldn't care less about your past, baby. You're a queen, and anytime you're with me, you'll be treated like one," Flea said with certainty.

"What about Dirty?" she asked. Her feelings were going every which way, and the weed wasn't making things no better.

"Leave him and get with me. I got you," Flea promised.

Midnight had to think about her options, and she let Flea know this. He didn't have a problem with it because he was one to just live in the moment.

After they finished talking, they got a suite on the twelfth floor. They'd both planned on making love to each other, but after taking showers, they just laid in each other's arms and went to sleep.

***

As soon as they got to the crib, Krash called Keebler in his office while the girls headed to bed.

"What's the word?" Keebler asked as he sat down.

"How are we going to deal with this Dirty issue?" Krash asked. He was starting to get a very bad vibe, and he always moved off what his instincts told him to do. He could see that Keebler was confused, so he explained how he was feeling.

"You know if and when he finds out about Midnight fucking Flea, it's going to be some shit. Then we still gotta deal with him and this Twin business," Krash said.

"Well, Flea is old enough to know what he's doing, and we've already warned him. All we can do is watch his back and hope he don't get caught up," Keebler replied. "As for Dirty, I think he understands the severity of the situation. The next move is on him, and I just hope he makes the right one," he continued.

"And if he doesn't?" Krash asked. He knew how Keebler felt about Dirty, as well as how hard it would be for him to push on him.

"If he doesn't do the right thing, then we gotta take him out," Keebler said after a long thought.

That was what Krash wanted to hear. Now he just wanted to lay it down for the rest of the night, and he knew Keebler could use some rest after being shot, so they called it a night.

*   *   *

Dirty was woken up the next morning by his phone ringing. He looked over to see if Midnight had come home but found her side of the bed empty. Sitting up in the bed, he looked at the phone, which now showed how many missed calls he had. As he scrolled down the list, the one number he was looking for didn't show up, but the last caller had him now fully awake as he called the number back.

"Tell me something good," Smoove answered on the third ring.

"I'm not going to take the job. I got too much going on right now," Dirty told him.

"So I hear. Maybe I can change your mind," Smoove said cheerfully as he sent the pictures his men took of him with Keebler and Krash at the hospital.

As Dirty looked at the pictures, he realized that the black Lincoln being followed by the two vans were the Black Gorilla Cartel following him. He got mad at the realization that he had been slipping like that, but he laughed it off.

"If this is supposed to shake me up, you must not know how I get down," Dirty said.

"If you're not with us, then you're against us," Smoove answered back.

"Is that a threat or a promise?" Dirty asked. "You know what? It don't even matter. Do what you gotta do, homie, but don't call my phone again," he continued and hung up before Smoove could say anything. "I can already tell this will be an eventful day," he told himself as he hopped out the bed and went to take a hot shower.

***

Keebler and Zya woke up to the smell of bacon flowing through the house. They got dressed and went to the kitchen to find Krash sitting at the kitchen table drinking a cup of hot coffee and Trina cooking breakfast.

"I thought you'd wanna sleep in and get some rest," Krash told Keebler as he sat down at the table.

"You know how I get down. I'll rest when I'm dead," Keebler told him. Zya poured him a cup of coffee and brought it to her man before going to help Trina make breakfast.

"You know we need to go find Twin," Krash stated firmly.

"No doubt," Keebler answered. "Today is his last day on this earth one way or the other," he continued.

"I need to go change," Zya said from the stove.

"You and Trina go get some clothes in my car, then come back to the crib," Keebler told her.

"And no hanging out having a girls day," Krash spoke up, but he was talking to Trina.

"Yes, dear," Trina replied without any fuss. She already knew what that meant. There was about to be a war in the streets, and they didn't want the girls to get caught up in the mix.

18

When Dirty finally jumped in the streets, he headed straight to North Memphis to holler at Twin. When he pulled up on the block, the street looked totally different from the day before. All the crime scene tape was now gone, and the strip was wide open like nothing happened. Dirty parked in front of the traphouse and found his cousin on the portch smoking a blunt.

"I see you up early," Twin said with a crooked smile.

"And I see you don't know how to listen," Dirty said as he stepped up on the porch. Truth be told, he already knew Twin wouldn't listen to him.

"I heard what you said," Twin admitted. "They gone have to show me something, though. I can't just stop getting money because some old niggas wanna see me," he continued. They continued going back and forth without realizing they were being watched from up the street.

Somehow, the black Lincoln managed to blend in without appearing suspicious. As soon as Dirty pulled up on the scene, the driver made the call to Smoove.

"Make sure you don't lose him again or it'll be your bodies they find riddled with bullets," Smoove told the men and hung up.

The hit team was on the way with strict instructions to kill on sight. That meant no matter where Dirty was when they pulled up or who he was with, everything and everybody got dealt with. The lookouts just prayed that they didn't lose sight of Dirty before the hit team got there.

***

An hour after eating breakfast, Krash and Keebler were leaving the house with enough artillery in the backseat to shoot up the entire North Memphis, which was where they were headed once Keebler found a vehicle to do the dirty work in. For some reason, Krash was getting that bad vibe again, and he almost went back to the house. It took everything in him to keep going, but he did.

Keebler found a blue Dodge Charger parked at a Wal-Mart, so he quickly hot-wired it and sped off. They headed straight to the north side without even stopping to put the rifles in the steamer. Once they got to the area, Krash found a safe restaurant to park his car. He grabbed all the artillery and hopped in the passenger seat of the Charger. As usual,

Keebler sped off before his best friend had the door closed good. There was nothing said because there was nothing to say. The mission was to kill Twin and whoever else got in the way.

***

It took the hit team no time to get to Scutterfield and find out the target was still at the same spot. When the vans swerved on the block, everything else happened so fast that it was like it all went in slow motion. By the time Dirty reacted to the action, it was too late. The side doors on both vans swung open, and four men jumped out of each van armed with choppers.

"Watch out!" Dirty yelled as he tried to take cover, but he had nowhere to run. The hit team quickly spread out, surrounding the traphouse to prevent any escape, then took care of business.

Bloc! Bloc! Bloc! Bloc! Bloc! Bloc! Bloc! Bloc! Bloc! Bloc!

The sounds of the rifles were terrifying, but the actual action looked like a scene from a gangster movie. One by one, people were being mowed down by the rapid gunfire. Dirty managed to get to the side of the house before he took several shots all over his body, killing him instantly. Twin never made it off the porch. A single shot to the head was all it took to take his life. When the hit team finally pulled off, junkies and dopeboys were all laid out on the street dead.

***

Just a couple of blocks away, Keebler pulled the steamer to the curb because they could hear the rapid gunfire.

"Looks like somebody beat us to the punch," Krash said, getting that vibe again.

To his surprise, instead of going on with the move, Keebler suggested they come back another time. He turned around, then headed back to where the Crown Vic was parked. They rode right past the black Lincoln and didn't think to check the rearview mirrors. When they got to the car, Krash put the rifles back in the back seat before getting behind the wheel while Keebler wiped the Charger down for any prints left behind. He got back to the car and smiled, but movement out the corners of his eyes quickly made the smile disappear.

***

"Ain't that the guy Smoove is looking for?" the driver of the black Lincoln asked. The passenger was currently on the phone with Smoove, so after he confirmed that it was indeed Keebler, he asked the boss what he wanted them to do.

"Go ahead and finish this so we can head home," Smoove ordered and ended the call.

They began following the Charger and spotted it as it pulled up at a restaurant. They noticed the Crown Vic as one of the vehicles from the night before. Instead of waiting, they sent word to the hit team to handle the business while they found a safe place to park. The vans swerved up on the Crown Vic, and the team hopped out just as they did at the traphouse.

Bloc! Bloc! Bloc! Bloc! Bloc! Bloc! Bloc! Bloc!

They shot the car up until it looked like swiss cheese, making sure the target was not moving when they finished. The vans sped off, leaving the black Lincoln there to make sure there were no survivors.

*   *   *

Back at the Peabody Hotel, Flea and Midnight had just woken up and were now watching a breaking news report that had all the local stations on alert. Midnight immediately got a bad feeling as they listened to the reporter.

"A double shooting in North Memphis has local police stunned. They got a call that two vans pulled up on Bickford Avenue, where a shooting occurred just the day before. Minutes later, calls came in about another shooting at Alizé's Soul Food Cabin located on Chelsea Avenue. Witnesses from both scenes say two vans filled with men are behind this act of terror," the reporter said, but that wasn't what had both of their attentions. The scene on Bickford showed the black BMW that was now shot to pieces, and the other scene showed the Crown Victoria full of holes parked at the restaurant.

THE END

COMING SOON!
AIN'T NO PITY

1

It was the beginning of a new year, and the day a killer was being released from prison. Philandis, A.K.A. Flatline, was convicted of two pistol charges after a group of men testified against him, stating that he was the person going around town murdering people. Although police originally charged Flatline with the murders, one-by-one the charges all got dismissed due to lack of evidence, and all that was left to convict the man were the charges for the pistols he got caught with. That was ten years ago. Now, the man was being released after serving his full sentence.

Getting off the Greyhound bus, Flatline quickly checked out his surroundings before spotting several payphones on the wall. Without thinking, he went to the phone and dialed numbers. He waited a few seconds before someone answered.

"Hello," the voice said with a country accent that almost made the man hang up.

"What's up, stranger?" Flatline asked with a smile once he recognized the voice. This time, it was the caller who got quiet, and this made him smile more.

"I take it you out since you calling me from a local number," the man said.

"Yep. I just touched down, and I can use a ride," Flatline told him.

"Where you at?" the man asked. Flatline let him know that he was at the Greyhound bus station and his partner promised that he was on the way.

Fifteen minutes later, Flatline was standing outside the bus station watching the different vehicles that cruised by when a silver four-door Dodge Ram sitting on 26-inch Chrome rims pulled up and stopped in front of him. Flatline stepped back, unsure of what to expect as the passenger side window rolled down.

"You need a lift stranger?" the guy asked country-like.

"My mafucking dawg, E-Bird," Flatline said with a smile as he hopped in the truck. As soon as he had the door closed good, E-Bird sped off.

E-Bird was Flatline's best friend and had been since junior high school. They hooked up after Flatline had his crew jump the man, and to his surprise, E-Bird didn't back down, even though he was outnumbered. Flatline liked his style, so he had his goons to stand down, and he approached the man. They'd been the best of friends ever since.

"I got something in the ashtray for you," E-Bird said as he rode down Hwy 82. Flatline looked and saw a bag of weed and a box of cigars.

"I see you think you still know me," Flatline said, smiling as he immediately rolled one up.

"I do know you, which is why there's another present for you under the seat," E-Bird said and watched as Flatline cautiously reached and pulled out a Glock 19x. It was at that time he noticed E-Bird had the same pistol laying across his lap.

"I knew you would probably wanna get on some gangsta shit as soon as you got out. It's the only reason I didn't take it upon myself to handle your light weight," he continued.

"I see you do know me," Flatline said as he nodded.

E-Bird took the time to catch him up on things, like how the streets were run, who ran what neighborhood, and what was hot in the dope game. Flatline listened as they passed the blunt back and forth, but his mind was on one thing at the moment, and that was getting revenge on Kwasi for testifying against him on the bogus murder charges. They had gotten so wrapped up in their conversation that Flatline didn't notice they had hit the south end until they were pulling up in the Southside Garden Apartments.

"Kwasi still dwell out here?" Flatline asked as E-Bird parked the truck.

"He's still over here hustling," E-Bird replied as they hopped out. He led the way through one of the cuts that took them through the apartments, and Flatline couldn't help but notice they were headed to the other side of the apartments.

"The track has moved over the years, but other than that, ain't too much changed out here," E-Bird continued just as they came out into a parking lot. "There's you boy right there," E-Bird pointed out as he nodded toward a group of men standing out on the other side of the lot.

For a minute, Flatline just stared at the man who broke the code and was standing around as if he hadn't done anything wrong. He quickly surveyed the area as he found the best way to get close to Kwasi.

"E, I need a diversion," Flatline said suddenly.

"Just let me know what I need to do," E-Bird said and listened as Flatline included him in his plan. E-Bird nodded and disappeared back through the cut while Flatline ducked back off and waited. He didn't have to wait long before the truck pulled up on the block with the system bumping.

Just as Flatline hoped, everyone out was watching the truck and admiring how clean it was, and this gave Flatline enough time to calmly step out of the cut and approach his target. Nobody seemed to be paying him any attention until it was too late. Kwasi was the first person to notice and recognize Flatline. His intuition said to yell for help since the man already had a pistol in his hand, but he never got the opportunity. Flatline raised the Glock, aimed and pulled the trigger, every shot hitting Kwasi square in the chest and knocking him off his feet. Kwasi was dead before his body hit the concrete.

As soon as the shots rang out, everyone ran for cover, and E-Bird sped off like he was scared. When people started noticing it was Kwasi who was being shot, they returned fire at the figure that was now running off through the cut. E-Bird knew where Flatline was headed, so he went back to where he originally parked and caught his best friend cautiously coming through the cut. Flatline hopped in the truck, and E-Bird sped off.

"I think we need to leave the city for a while," E-Bird said as he headed for the highway. Flatline didn't really care what else they did. He finally got his revenge on Kwasi for getting on the stand and lying on him.

"Roll up another blunt to ease our minds," E-Bird said, pulling Flatline out of his daydream. "So, what's the plan now?" E-Bird asked suddenly.

Flatline continued rolling up as he spoke his mind. "I want to form a hit squad and take over the city," he explained.

E-Bird just drove and listened, unsure how to tell his best friend that the game had changed over the years. Neighborhoods were run by cliques, and the police were known to look the other way at certain times.

The blunt got in rotation, and by the time Flatline realized they were headed to Lake Village, the murder he had committed seemed like a thing of the past.

As they crossed the Arkansas bridge and hit some neighborhood streets, Flatline could not help but notice how good the city of Lake Village looked now. Compared to the city of Greenville, it looked and felt like two different worlds. E-Bird pulled up at the house, and it finally felt like Flatline was home.

"I see you've kept the crib up," he said as they hopped out the truck.

"Wait until you see the inside," E-Bird with a smile that made Flatline wonder.

As soon as they went in the house, Flatline immediately noticed the changes. E-Bird had renovated the entire inside of the house.

"Wait until you see your room," E-Bird said and led the way to the back of the house.

***

Back in Greenville, the scene was chaotic in the Southside Garden Apartments. Police were everywhere, trying to make sense of the dead body that lay surrounded by homeboys attempting to hide the body. Word had already spread around the area that Kwasi was dead, and it had now gotten to the white projects where Kima and Tricie were known to hustle.

"Girl, did you hear that shit about Kwasi?" Kima asked after making another weed sale.

"I heard but I don't believe it," Tricie said. She knew the man kept a team around him at all times, so getting at him wouldn't have been that easy.

After a few minutes, someone yelled "Police," and everybody in the projects cleared the block.

"Let's ride through the Southside Garden and see what we can find out," Kima suggested. Since the police were now in the area, it didn't seem like a bad idea. They both hopped in Tricie's Equinox and sped out of the apartments.

When they pulled up at the Southside Garden, the police presence was so thick that Tricie had to park at the neighborhood store, and they walked back to the apartments. Kima led the way through the cut that led to the track, and they bumped into a man who ran with Kwasi named Kojak.

"Kojak, is it true about Kwasi?" Tricie asked the man who once had a huge crush on her.

"Yeah, they ran up and gunned him down like a rabid animal," Kojak told her, then broke down crying.

"Do you know who did it?" Kima asked the million-dollar question.

Kojak looked up at her with pure hatred because he knew who she was related to. "They say Philandis did it," Kojak said through clinched teeth.

Tricie took a step back at the mention of Flatline, but Kima held her ground. "That can't be true. Philandis is still locked up," Kima said loudly, even though she was talking mainly to herself.

"Well, just in case he is out, you let him know that we coming for his ass," Kojak got up in her face and said before walking off.

"Let's dip before we end up in something that ain't got shit to do with us," Kima told Tricie, who had a look of pure terror on her face.

Since Kojak went one way, they went the other and headed back to the car.

***

Back in Arkansas, E-Bird opened the last bedroom door and led the way inside. Flatline used to always sleep in that room whenever he stayed over, but as he stepped inside, he could see it wasn't the same room. Inside was a California king-sized bed with a 60-inch flat screen TV mounted on the wall in front of the bed. All Flatline could do for the moment was stare around the room because he didn't think he was coming home to much, but the truth of the matter was, if he didn't have anyone else, he had E-Bird.

"I still have another surprise for you," E-Bird said as he went over to the dresser and opened the drawers, then opened the closet door. "I took the liberty of getting you a fresh wardrobe," he said with a genuine smile.

"How did you know what I'd like?" Flatline asked as he went to the closet and checked out the gear.

"You're my brother. I got you the latest designer shit I knew you'd like," E-Bird said truthfully.

Flatline walked over to where E-Bird was now standing at the door and gave the man a hug. "Thanks, bruh," Flatline whispered before letting him go.

"How about you go shower and get out of those tight-ass clothes so we can hit the town?" E-Bird suggested. Flatline glanced at his attire, and for the first time, he realized he still had on the clothes the prison gave him, and this made him smile. "I'll be up front," E-Bird said and left Flatline alone.

***

Kojak made it to his car safely and pulled out of the Southside Gardens. What he'd heard was constantly replaying over in his head.

"It looked like Philandis," the man said once the shooting had stopped.

Now, he was thinking about what Kima had told him in the cut.

"That can't be true. Philandis is still locked up," Kima pleaded.

"For his sake, he better still be locked up because if he shows his face in the hood, I'll make sure he loses his life," Kojak said to himself as he tried to drive, wipe the tears from his face, and dial numbers on his phone at the same time.

"What's up, Kojak?" the young voice replied happily on the phone.

"Get everybody together and meet me at your pad. We need to have an emergency meeting, Nap," Kojak said. "And in case you don't know already, somebody just took out Kwasi right in front of us," he continued to let Nap know what the meeting was about, and how serious it was.

"Pull up on me," Nap said and ended the call.